WESTSIDE HARPY

MIDLIFE OLYMPIANS #2

T.J. DESCHAMPS

EDITED BY
PATRICIA LONG

For my kids. All the long hours and hard work I put in to these books is so I may leave a legacy you'll be proud of and hopefully a few bucks in royalties to split between the three of you after I'm gone. Blow it on something fun.
Love,
Mami, Maman, Mother, Mooooooom

INTRODUCTION

I've always found religion a fascinating topic. Mythology is religion and I tried to treat it with reverence. Well, with as much reverence as a blasphemous non-believer with a smidgeon of religious trauma can muster.

There is no such thing as a uniform form of belief. Even with well known religious texts, the details will vary from city to city and author to author.

This author would like to say this is a fictional world and based on Greco-Roman beliefs, but is by no means an academic text. So, I've created my own world with its own rules. Parentage and familial lines are set up for what works best for my plot.

I'd also like to add, that in my fictional world Midlife Olympians, harpy isn't an insult and they aren't nasty creatures. Harpy is a badge of honor. Mighty warriors. Just like I depicted sirens in the Midlife Supernaturals series (and these books, too).

I used a team of editors, but typos happen. If you see a typo and want to help out, please send the page and line number to author@tammydeschamps.com

You're also welcome to email me if you liked the book, too.

PROLOGUE

Thetis opened her eyes. Raging against her fate, she wished she could shut them against this infernal nightmare. The nymph had to admit the scene was more peaceful than she'd imagined this place to be. The air was fragrant with the scent of asphodel. Shades of mortals drifted in the meadow. Shades of water nymphs played on the shores and swam the river. The River Lethe, making them forget the troubles of the living world. The firmament, the eternal twilight of Hades, twinkled above. She didn't want to be here, but there would be no escape. The dead never left the Underworld.

A hand clasped her shoulder. It was warm and firm, fleshy, and yet tremendous power simmered just beneath the skin. Only a deity felt that way.

She should know. Thetis had been the consort of a few. The latest had been a mistake. She saw that now as his living flesh gripped what remained of her life force.

"We must act quickly," his deep voice urged. "You must hide in Tartarus before they detect your shade's presence here."

She turned to her erstwhile coconspirator and lover. She was supposed to be beyond feeling. Still, anger, hurt, and betrayal tangled like a knot of sharp-thorned vines within her, springing forth in three words.

"You killed me."

"You failed. Lydia is still in the hands of the Olympians," the god drawled. "I told you there'd be consequences."

"Thank you. It's more than you did for Dione, letting her take the fall for you." She hoped that barb would sting. Unlike her unrequited feelings, he'd loved and admired the Titan—or so she thought.

Anger sparked in his eyes like twin flames, there and gone. He scoffed. "She was never part of it."

The information shocked Thetis. She'd been working under the assumption the Titan was helping them. Dione had more reasons than the rest of the group of conspirators to want the Titans free. She hadn't seen her children in eons.

The dead water nymph looked away, turning her gaze at the swimming shades of dead sister nymphs. How many of them were fodder to some lusty god who took things too far? At least she died trying to become more than a deity's whore. She was done with their bullshit machinations.

"I helped you because you promised me godhood once the plan was complete. What's my motivation to not spill everything to Persephone and Hades?"

The god's beautifully carved face sharpened to deadly angles. "I think there's someone you should meet."

The hand tightened its grip. The landscape spun. They were in a different part of the Underworld. A shade that seemed too thin to be a full shade stood next to the gate to Tartarus. She pressed her hands against the black pillar. Insubstantial, they passed through glittering onyx.

"You can't access that anymore, Apollonia," the god called.

The shade turned. The former Oracle's black eyes without sclerae or irises narrowed. She spat a single word, "You."

The god laughed, mocking in its heartiness. "Who am I?"

Apollonia scowled, and then tears slid down her ethereal cheeks. They were the color of blood. "Echidna brought me to you, but I don't remember why. I don't even remember your name."

The shade of the former Oracle flickered in and out of existence. Each reappearance thinner than the last.

"That's because I broke your mind for not going through with what I told you to do. The little crack wasn't enough." The god turned his back to Apollonia, dismissing her with the action, and faced Thetis. "There's not much a shattered shade can tell anyone. Enough motivation?"

Thetis didn't want to go to Tartarus, but Apollonia's fate was much worse. The nymph still possessed a mostly solid form, and her memories were intact. It was almost like being alive. Almost.

"What do you want of me while I'm there?" she asked, smiling. She hoped her pretty smile still had the same affect it had on gods when she was alive.

"Tell all who will hear. The mortal world is hurting and looking for new gods. Tell them if they accept me as their leader, we'll overthrow their captors together, then we'll go for the Angelic Anocracy. With them out of the way, we'll become more powerful than ever."

Thetis bowed her head, hiding her grin of triumph. She'd give the Titans the message alright. Except, she'd place herself in the place of their queen. She'd start by finding the sea Titans, Scylla and Charybdis.

CHAPTER
ONE

Nothing like waking up to a good cup of coffee and a nightmare. A spider the size of a corgi skittered in my direction across the linoleum of the kitchen floor. A few weeks ago, I would've screamed bloody murder at the sight of the creature. If you're an arachnophobe and wish to conquer your fear, I highly suggest living with Arachne and her children as a form of immersion therapy.

Maybe not.

If you're not a good person, you might end up as their dinner.

Cerberus lifted his three heads, one woofed, another sneeze-drooled (don't ask, it's even grosser than you'd imagine), and the third panted, not seeming to understand why the other two heads were in a tizzy.

"It's okay, Spot," I said, but my tone lacked the confidence I attempted to portray.

Cerberus's heads whined, panted, and drooled respectively. Then the pooch rose, circled around in his dog bed and settled down again.

At first, I felt ridiculous calling the three-headed monster "Spot."

Upon Persephone's instruction, I had to call Cerberus the name while outside her domain. I wasn't clear why, but she was adamant. Never argue with the Queen of the Underworld, not unless you want to end up her subject.

Like Arachne and her children, I'd grown accustomed to his name over the last few months. Also, he acted like a dumb dog someone would name "Spot" ninety percent of the time.

The spider spun wildly. Something was stuck to his back, likely a sticky note from Arachne.

"Stop spinning, please."

The spider obeyed.

I was right. There was a note attached to his back. In neat blue script contrasting the yellow paper, the note read, "Be down in five."

A totally unnecessary communication. Arachne liked testing my patience with her children.

The spider tapped one of its legs impatiently. Gregory was the peskiest of the pest babies.

"Okay, Greg. I read it. You can go back to your mother now."

The spider spun in a circle. It was definitely Gregory. Most of the children would go back to Arachne, satisfied. Greg didn't trust me, or he didn't like the paper on his back. Either way, he'd keep spinning near my feet until I took the note off him.

I shuddered, reaching then drawing back my hand.

The action excited Greg. His spinning became more frantic.

The thing was, I could tolerate his presence, mostly, but *touching* the spider was a whole other story. However, if I didn't take the note, there was a good possibility that he would take it upon himself to crawl up my leg. The thought alone made my vision swim and darken around the edges. I really didn't want to pass out in my own home. Again.

I inhaled deeply, closing my eyes. "One, two..."

"Thanks, Greg," my son Luke said, followed by the telltale sound of paper crinkling.

Clicking sounds indicated the spider was scurrying off.

I opened one eye, hoping that to be the case.

Lukie had the note in hand, a smirk on his handsome face. When my son gave me that sarcastic smirk, he looked like my ex, Carlo—or rather Pietro now that he was in jail and using his birth name. I'd known him as Carlo for too long to go back to the name of the boy I'd fallen in love with.

After I'd fallen out of love with Carlo, I'd broken the cardinal rule of criminals: never snitch. I'd told the ISEA agents everything I knew about my ex to save my own skin. It's a stupid rule. No one in real life followed it. There was no honor among thieves or any of that nonsense.

Besides, Carlo had done worse than snitch before I even had the chance. He'd made up things about me. He'd pinned all his crimes his crew had ever done on me, claiming I was a supe and had mind-controlled them since I was sixteen years old.

Pfft.

If I could do that, could someone please explain his multiple extramarital affairs, why he and his crew stole my savings, and most of all why he ditched me once he made the biggest score of his life. Can't? Neither could the lawyers.

Faking that I was psychic may have made me a bit of a scam artist myself, but I'd never committed a serious crime. Not really. Telling people what they wanted to hear and giving them advice under the guise of being able to read the future wasn't illegal, *yet.*

The government was talking about passing laws about that now that supernaturals or "supes" had come out of the closet as real. There were a lot of charlatans out there pretending to be supes to game people out of their money. How did you prove someone was not psychic?

People had a hard time telling when I couldn't see the future. My heart was always in the right place when I fabricated readings. I gave good advice and entertained them in the process.

A few months ago, I discovered that I'd descended from the Oracles of Delphi and could read the tapestry woven for humanity by the Fates. I just had no recollection of any of my real predictions. So, still a fake psychic, but kinda not?

My son set the sticky note with a few spider fibers still attached on the table and then turned, opening the coffee mug cupboard. "I think Arachne sends Gregory so you'll get over your phobia."

"I think she sends Greg because she finds my phobia amusing."

Luke chuckled as he poured some of the steaming coffee into his mug. "You've got to admit it's kind of funny that an arachnophobe lives with Arachne and her children."

"Says the guy who asked for a tarantula every birthday."

Juan, Luke's fiancé, entered the kitchen. Ready for his commute to work, Juan sported a blue velvet smoking jacket, cream button up, and trousers. His lovely curls were on display, shiny and expertly coifed. He flashed us a thousand-watt smile. Juan was definitely a looker. Then again, so was my Luke.

"Buenos dias, familia."

"Ah, my favorite is awake. Kalimera!"

"I love when you speak Greek, mami. It sounds so beautiful." He kissed me on each cheek like a proper son-in-law should. I loved Juan fiercely; he was so good for my boy. I couldn't wait until the two tied the knot. Unlike some parents, I kept it to myself.

My heart had grown two sizes since they moved into the house in Milagro Bay. I was just happy to be a part of their lives.

"Don't let him tease you. He doesn't like spiders either. He just hides it better," Juan whispered conspiratorially.

I pointed at my grown son. "Ha!"

"Not true. I love them!" Luke placed his hand over his heart, mock offended, but mischief sparkled in his eyes. "Ask Greg."

I shuddered. I wouldn't be asking any spider anything.

My son and future son-in-law chuckled and then kissed each other.

"Aw!"

"Ma, stop!" Luke blushed.

"Love is nothing to be ashamed of."

Affection was something I'd only experienced in the early days with Carlo. Our marriage had chilled with each affair. So much so, my ex would teasingly call me roomie. It stung. Every. Time.

I hoped the boys would stay true to each other. Even a modicum of loyalty was better than what I had with my ex.

Juan poured a to-go cup.

Luke got Juan's bento lunchbox ready to carry out the door.

I loved watching their little routine as I sipped my coffee.

"I put some of that leftover lamb souvlaki you liked in there," I said.

Luke groaned. "Ma! He was fine with the tabouli I made."

"I really am, babe." Juan kissed my son again and winked his thanks in my direction before exiting to the back porch.

Unlike my Luke, Juan was not a vegetarian. I'd slip him meat whenever I could. Luke called it undermining their healthy lifestyle, I called it giving the skinny man a little extra before he wasted away.

"It's such a long commute to Seattle from Milagro Bay. Too bad he can't work from home like you, Lukie."

He threw up his hands. "For goodness' sake, ma. It's Luke."

I grinned. "Okay, Luke."

I liked to tease him with his nickname, but I'd never disrespect him and call him by his dead name. Never accepting our son, Carlo refused to call him Luke.

They hadn't spoken in ten years. Ever since Luke had moved into his college dorm. My son kept in touch with me, but I hadn't seen him face-to-face in all that time.

I should've left Carlo a long time ago and followed Luke out west. I could've started over years ago. Now, I was eking out a new life in a new town as a middle-aged woman.

There were a thousand reasons why I should've left Carlo. I just couldn't bring myself to leave the man who stuck with me. Some good my loyalty did. In the end, he left me.

Luke looked at his watch and gulped down the rest of his coffee. "Got to go. Grandma is picking me up for harpy lessons."

Nicky, the local queen of the harpies, was my stepmother. Since my birth mother Apollonia faked her death and married Nicky after she'd abandoned her previous life, the harpy didn't have a hand in raising me nor was a part of Luke's childhood. However, Nicky had always wanted to be part of our lives. She stepped in wonderfully as my mother-figure and Luke's grandma.

Wanting to see Nicky too, I followed Luke to the back door.

She flew in just as we walked out. As a full-blooded harpy, she was born with golden wings and soft golden down, covering her lithe humanoid form.

We greeted her with hugs.

She tousled his hair affectionately. "Ready, Lukie?"

Nicky got to call him that and only Nicky.

He grinned ear to ear. "Yeah. I'm hoping to sprout some wings."

"Sorry, kiddo, very few harpies not born with wings can do that."

"My boy is a prodigy," I said, partly because I thought so and partly because I wanted to be included in the conversation. The little girl my mother left behind ached for time with Nicky.

"Your lessons will come soon," she said, wrapping her arms around Luke.

I nodded, hating that I felt a twinge of jealousy. I didn't know which I was jealous of more: my stepmom getting Luke all day or Luke getting a day with the mom I'd always wanted. At forty-four, it was pretty pathetic to be jealous of either.

TWO

When I returned to the kitchen, I found a monster and a god having breakfast. Fortunately, both were expected to be there since they lived with me.

From the waist up, Arachne could be anyone's grandma. A thin, elderly woman, she kept her silver curls under a yellow head-scarf dotted with cornflowers. She wore cat-eye glasses with a chain so she wouldn't lose them. A large, floor-length muumuu the same pattern as the scarf covered her round spider lower body and eight spindly legs. I'd never seen her without the muumuu and hoped I never would.

While Arachne's appearance gave me the chills, her personality was kind—at least to me and Luke. In our short friendship, she'd proven herself loyal, fighting and bleeding for me in more ways than one.

Sitting across from her, Hermes's appearance gave me the opposite of the chills. He had the kind of body that had inspired sculptors for thousands of years. A face only the best painter could capture. Strong jaw, chiseled cheekbones, dark eyes with long, curling lashes, and the best head of black curly hair I'd ever sank fingers into. His nose was typical Grecian, and my favorite part of his face. Did I mention he had marvelous hands and a supple mouth?

My face heated. We had taken things slow, getting to know each other without including the bedroom yet. I was the one holding us back there. I'd been with one man for thirty years, not to mention rejected and cheated on. Intimacy didn't come easy.

Also, Hermes wanted to play for keeps. He didn't want us consummating anything until I was sure I was in for the long haul.

Since the ink was barely dry on my divorce papers, I didn't know if I could commit again so soon.

Finally noticing me standing there, ogling my boyfriend, both looked up.

"Gregory thinks you don't like him," Arachne said, knitting needles working on yet another doily.

Oh boy, the guilt for not loving her babies was starting early this morning.

"I like him well enough—for a spider." I managed only one shudder, so I was improving.

Hermes chuckled. "At least it's not spiders *and* snakes."

I shot him a nasty look.

Arachne reared her head, indignant. "Don't compare my children to Echidna's slithering brats."

On my way out west, I ran into two Titans who had escaped Tartarus. Echidna and Typhon, two nightmares on snake tails, had wanted to use me to open the gates of Tartarus, all the way, to free the rest of the Titans. They'd killed my mother and many of my ancestors trying. I don't think they knew how the gate worked, but for some reason, they thought my line could open it. They had gotten away when Nicky and the harpies stepped in.

The Olympians were working on a third Titan on the scheme. Dione had been my first contact with the supernatural, informing me of my powers and my inheritance, so I was a little sad she'd turned out a false friend.

Hermes held up his hands. "I didn't."

"You two about ready?"

Arachne nodded. "Yep. Just grabbing some coffee and breakfast."

"Did I miss the kids?" Hermes asked, not hiding the disappointment in his voice.

I gave him a rueful smile. "Sorry."

The god, never having a 9-5, went to bed when he tired and rose when he had enough rest. Business professionals, the adult "kids" were early risers—a concept Hermes grasped but would likely never apply to himself.

I was a late riser myself, but this priestess gig involved a lot. Especially since I had to learn everything about being one. Today wasn't a lesson day. I would act as Oracle to mundanes at the temple. My mother had run a divination shop out of the front of the house. A recent rise in Neo-Greco-Roman belief made that impossible for me to do. The numbers were too many. I only served locals in the little shop twice a month.

The clock over the oven read seven. "The mundane pilgrims should be making their way up the mountain now."

I didn't want to get there after the worshippers.

Arachne stuffed her doily and knitting needles somewhere in her muumuu. "Neo-Greco-Romanists need to learn the concept of waiting on the priestesses, not the other way around. No sacrifices, no groveling, just give me this and help me with that."

I shrugged. "With every pantheon revealed as real, the Olympians have more competition than in the olden days."

Mundanes picked and chose their gods the way they used to choose restaurants, trying out different religions just to see which ones benefitted them the most. I was the go-between, so the gods didn't get offended.

Hermes seemed to be the only one who realized he wasn't what he once was. The few interactions I had with the rest of the Twelve proved they were akin to washed up rock stars, who thought they could make a new album and still hit the top forty. Everyone has heard of them, but did anyone really want to buy the new album?

"Well, I guess we better get you two to the temple to serve the ingrates," Hermes said, the corners of his mouth fighting a grin.

He emptied his mug and washed it by hand. Arachne poured the remainder of her coffee into a to-go mug. I mentally prepared myself to travel via a ley line or what he liked to call the Backroads.

Hermes explained that my realm—or what I called a universe—was one of many. Kind of like a singular bubble in a sea of foam. Connecting the bubbles were roads that Hermes, or a planeswalker like Phyr, could travel.

His explanation sounded a lot like string theory, I think, but my knowledge of theoretical physics and the multiverse was whatever I gleaned from PBS before nodding off in front of the television.

Hermes wrapped an arm around my waist and held Arachne's hand. The spider-woman could run as fast as Hermes through the cold, airless roads. Cerberus also ran along with us, able to cross without Hermes.

The Backroads looked like they were set in a video game. Streams of different colored lights shot through the dark. I pressed my face into his neck, not wanting to get vertigo from the speed and swirling lights.

The god came to an abrupt halt, setting me down.

It took a moment to get my legs which had turned to jelly to function and work the kinks out of my back. We were in the back room of the temple, where we kept our temple wardrobe and accoutrements.

Arachne skittered ahead to change behind a screen into a chiton. She'd woven all our temple vestments.

Cerberus found his usual cushion, circled it and settled down.

Alone, Hermes used the opportunity to snatch me up again and press a kiss on my lips.

I'm not going to lie. Every single time the god kissed me, I was surprised anew that he wanted to. Someday I'd get used to that, to him kissing me, but I doubt I'd ever get used to the *way* he kissed me. Hermes was all in. His kisses felt like my lips were the first and last thing he thought about each day. Today he put even more into it. As if he wanted to savor every second.

When we broke apart, I said, "That felt like goodbye. Aren't you staying?"

He gave me a sheepish grin and scratched the back of his neck, apology in his eyes. "It's time to report to my father."

Part of Hermes's agreement with Zeus to take a sabbatical on Earth was to report to him on the progress of the new oracle, which was me. He was also assigned to stay as my protector. Echidna and Typhon, my erstwhile Titan abductors, were still on the loose.

"Will you see Dione?"

He shrugged. "Doesn't matter if I do or don't. She hasn't spoken. She refuses. Nothing has worked. The only thing the Olympians can do about it is set her in a place like Tartarus. We can't return her there, if there's a way to break out."

"Tell her I know why she did it. Why she sacrificed so many oracles."

He reared his head. "Why?"

"Her children. They're in Tartarus. Even after Dione refused to fight in the Titanomachy, your father imprisoned them." It was a guess based on what I'd seen in snippets of my ancestor's memories.

The god actually blanched.

Well, score one to me for frightening an ancient powerful being.

"My father would have considered his children with her as gods, not Titans."

"If your father didn't imprison them, who did?"

Hermes took a deep breath, dark eyebrows furrowing. "Maybe he did. The war was hard, we were fighting our own kin, and I was a young god at the time. The conflict took a lot out of me emotionally. I'd assumed my half siblings died or lived out their lives in this realm, fading as some of the more obscure gods have."

Guess it wasn't just human families who kept secrets. How terrible for him. "I'm sorry. This is your life, and I'm treating it as a legend." I then gave Hermes a hug.

He kissed the top of my head. "Don't fret. It all happened very long ago. You have the kindest heart to worry about my feelings."

"Of course, I do." I met his gaze. "I care about you."

His eyes were warm and brown, and they twinkled when I told him how I felt. He brushed a thumb along my jawline and over my lips. "I need to look into Dione's children's whereabouts. I'll try to be back today. If I'm not, can you ask the harpies to take you back?"

I frowned in response.

Hermes lifted my chin with the crook of his finger. "I'm sorry to do this, Lydia. I know you want to investigate, too, but your duties are here. If her children are in Tartarus, and Dione is trying to get them out, there stands a chance that someone wants her to fail. That puts you in danger."

"And Luke."

"And Luke," he agreed.

So far, no Olympians knew about my son's oracle powers, except Hermes. Luke wanted everything to do with being a harpy and nothing to do with the temple and being a priest. For reasons he hadn't explained, Hermes hadn't outed my kid to his father.

The harpies would keep Luke's oracle powers to themselves. I hadn't known them long, but it was clear they watched out for their own and considered my son and I harpies, despite our distinct lack of harpy features. The harpies' loyalty to each other outweighed their loyalty to Hades and definitely outweighed any sentiments about loyalty to Olympus.

"I get it."

Hermes kissed me once more and gave me a lingering once-over, as if committing my image to memory, before disappearing.

CHAPTER

THREE

Changed into a blue chiton with a white zoster belted under *The Girls*, I examined myself in the mirror. I loved chitons, emphasized what I liked, let the rest be free and loose.

Behind me, Arachne arranged my curls in a golden hair net she called a kekryphalos, and then attached the net to a gold circlet of laurel leaves she'd place on the top of my head. She stepped back to admire her work. Her eyes dewed.

"Are you alright?" I asked, taking her hand in mine.

A smile spread on her lips. She dabbed her eyes with one of her self-woven kerchiefs. "Don't mind this old fool. I missed the ritual and pageantry involved around being a temple priestess and didn't know it."

I squeezed her hand.

"I'm glad you found me. I liked being a hotel manager, but this is my purpose. Serving the temple makes life fulfilling." She sighed heavily.

She'd served in a temple on Olympus, working directly for Athena. I don't know the details but there seemed to be a love trian-

17

gle. Arachne had fallen in love with Athena, Athena loved a gorgon—the details are fuzzy on which one. The gorgon planned on doing something nefarious or did something nefarious. Arachne wiped out the competition, righted the wrongdoing, and had a nice lunch in one fell swoop.

I know, I know. Gross and whoa, not cool, but she was an ancient monster from another world, not a human.

Athena must've held some sort of torch for Arachne too. Instead of executing my friend, the goddess of wisdom had her banished from Olympus. Arachne told me she wandered Greece for a bit, serving in temples there, but Christianity swept in a couple thousand years ago when a guy name Paul showed up in Athens. After that, Persephone had set Arachne up in different places to function as a hostess of one type or another, usually inns or halfway houses for supes. My friend had been a front desk manager for centuries, but her heart was in being a priestess.

"I'm glad Hermes decided to take me to your hotel." And convinced me I needed the monster. A true arachnophobe, I was originally terrified of the mother of spiders and wasn't too keen on bringing her on the road trip which led me here. Now, I was grateful Arachne decided to stay on as a priestess. Even if I had to tolerate her children once in a while.

"Hermes is a good one," Arachne smiled through her tears. "No history of being a groper like his siblings."

Such a low bar on Olympus. I sighed inwardly, I would keep my thoughts about that world and its standards to myself. Earth had enough problems to focus on.

I rose. "Alright. It's showtime."

The main area of the temple is kinda the same as the Temple of Apollo in Delphi back in the 8th century BCE—or so Arachne says. The temple where my ancestors served still exists today but only the ruins.

In the temple on Washington state's Mount Olympus, everything is made of Grecian marble, including large statues of The Twelve and small icons for a number of minor gods, which weren't in the original. Delphi was mostly about Apollo, but we were attracting bigger numbers and for the whole pantheon.

Petitioners, who drove in from wherever and hiked to get here, lined up outside between the Doric columns and down the marble steps.

I sat on a tripod chair just like the priestess Pythia and the rest of the oracles. Not the comfiest of seats but part of this job required carrying on ancient traditions. Either ancient oracles had tinier butts than mine or when there was more than oracle, they didn't have to sit forever and ever on the tiny perch.

To my right, a bronze canister of dried laurel leaves imported from Delphi sat. At my feet, a tiny man-made, narrow ravine circulated around the seat. For now, the trench was dry. As I settled my backside on the tripod and lifted the lid of the canister, Arachne skittered to a giant lever.

The first petitioners began to enter the oracle's chamber.

I tossed a handful of dried laurel leaves in my mouth, nodding to Arachne as I chewed. She pulled the lever.

A foggy liquid flowed from a spout on the wall behind me, filling the trench, circling the tripod and draining into the wall on the other side to be recycled. The reek of rotten eggs wafted into my nostrils. It was only the stink natural hot springs sometimes emitted, but I did *not* care for the odor.

The first petitioner was a young man in his early twenties. Clothes hung from his wiry frame.

I chewed and chewed. As soon as he touched my outreached hand, I'd lean forward and inhale a dose of the fumes.

He touched my hand. Taking a deep breath, I waited to go into my oracle trance. And waited. And waited.

Nothing happened.

Arachne scurried over, asking in Greek, "What's the holdup?"

"I don't know," I replied in the same language, keeping my face and tone as neutral as possible.

I couldn't control my predictions, but I thought I had the formula: laurel leaves, noxious fumes, touching the petitioner.

The petitioner must've gotten a good look at Arachne's lower half and started backing away. Gangly arms thrown protectively forward. "What *is* that?"

"Arachne is a priestess to the gods," I replied firmly, confused he didn't know who she was.

Harpies we had working the front of the temple warned that beings of Olympus were present inside. He was told by freaking harpies Arachne was here. If gold feathered women didn't freak him out, I had no patience for—

Movement in my periphery just beyond Arachne caught my eye. Something nightmarish blinked back at me. Or rather, some things. Three bearded men, adjoined at the waist, flashed smiles simultaneously.

I'm not particularly frightened of bearded men, but they aren't wearing clothes and just below the navel their torsos are connected to a red-scaled tail wrapped around a column.

What was it with monsters with snake tails and their obsession with me?

That may not have been the most productive thought when the three-headed man-snake was threatening "annihilation" and "doom" in ancient Greek—at least that's what I picked up.

Spiders by the dozen dispersed from Arachne's skirts. She shouted something. I picked up the word "daímonas" which was "daimon" in English. Daimons weren't necessarily evil but this one had Arachne up in arms.

The harpies on guard out front, protected the petitioners, corralling them away from the entrance.

"Spot!"

Cerberus shook his Labrador Retriever head, dropping the domestic dog illusion for the three-headed monster reality. He charged the column at the same time as Arachne's army of children dispersed from under her chiton.

The three-bodied nightmare on the Doric column spread white wings and took flight.

I shrieked, running but didn't know where to go.

Cerberus bounded off the column, loping after me. He caught the daimon's tail. The interloper flung my dog off. However, he was bleeding black blood all over my temple from where the monster pooch had bitten him.

Good dog.

All three heads incredulous as one of the torsos examined his wound. The monster said something to Arachne. This time with less venom in his tone.

Arachne replied and stuck out her tongue.

The daimon magicked away his wound and transformed into one man. Tall, handsome if you like curly black hair, beards, and built like a Spartan warrior with a sizeable package. Arms now reaching toward me, he said in modern Greek, "I only wanted to propose to you a partnership. Oh, great Oracle of the new Olympics."

"Spot, come to me," I commanded, not trusting the daimon. People on the up and up didn't sneak in the back.

Arachne folded her thin arms across her chest. "Partnership. Uh-huh. More like get her in bed, Nareas." She nodded at his unclothed dangly bits.

Nareas. I knew the name and recognized the daimon now, or at least when he was in his three-headed form. My grandparents had shown me pictures of his statue. He was a shapeshifting daimon but not a shapeshifter like the animal shifters.

"I meant no offense. I simply forgot mortal customs." He held up his hands. A blue peplos manifested, covering the warrior bod.

Thank goodness. I was no prude, and had no attraction to this daimon, but it's hard to keep your eyes on someone's face when they have parts swaying with their movements.

"What kind of partnership," I asked.

He flashed serrated white teeth. "I will help you with your predicament."

I schooled my face to appear neutral and kept my tone skeptical, as I countered, "What predicament is that?"

He made a show of looking in the direction where the devotees had stood. In a low voice, he said, "I've been watching you." He flashed me a sympathetic smile too studied to be real. "You don't know how to access your gift—or rather, Dione didn't tell you how to use it."

My heart lurched in my chest.

Arachne, Nicky, and Hermes hadn't said I needed training. None of the Olympians I'd spoken to mentioned it. I assumed Oracles innately knew how to use their powers.

Arachne swung her gaze in my direction. By the way her face dropped, I hadn't managed to keep schooling mine. She said nothing to me, returning her attention to Nareas. "What do you know of being the Oracle?"

"I'm always watching. I know a lot of secrets about a lot of gods and Titans. Secrets are currency. I know the secret of reading the Tapestry of the Fates."

Arachne scoffed. "It's an innate gift."

"True. You must be born with the ability, but even natural talent needs guidance. I know how Dione gave each oracle the knowledge they needed to be an effective oracle."

I recalled the reading of the thread already spun and woven for my ancestor following Dione through Hades to the gate of Tartarus. I'd assumed that the Titan was trying to use my long-gone relative to open the gate.

Did I have it all wrong? Was the knowledge there? She had been waiting here for me. Maybe Jen and Brad showing up had been a coincidence. If so, we'd made a grievous mistake sending her off to Olympus.

"What's in it for you?" I asked. I highly doubted his price would be small.

Nareas grinned. "I want in." He gestured to the statues. "I want a statue with my name on a placard for the petitioners. I want to be a god."

I took a step back. It wasn't a conscious choice. Carlo, my ex, always wanted more than he deserved, and he also wasn't shy to admit it.

"Yeah, right. Zeus will never go for that." Arachne cackled, the lower tier of her chiton wriggling with the movement.

The daimon cut the monstrous old lady a sharp look. His body trembled and lost partial solidity as he told her, "Zeus reigns in Olympus. We're here, and this is the Wild West where it's up to mortals, not gods, whether anyone is *in*. I just need a name and a placard; it won't take anything away from The Twelve by getting a piece of the adoration action."

I'd made the decision to be Oracle because I was in a tight spot. If I'd thought it through, I would've declined the position. In my hubris, I thought I could get out of the contract. I didn't want to rush into a decision again.

"I need until the next full moon to decide."

"Wise." Nereas sketched a bow. "Until the moon waxes, lovely one."

His body simply faded from sight.

"How long until the moon waxes?" I asked Arachne.

"Two weeks."

That gave me plenty of time to decide if I should trust Nareas. I could consult with Hermes and Nicky. Research whether he ever was involved with the oracles of the past. Maybe even visit Hades and talk Persephone into letting me see my mother again.

I didn't know the daimon, but I knew one thing. Making a deal with any supernatural creature who wanted to be a god would be my last resort.

FOUR

It took us a while to chase down the pilgrims and convince them that the intruder was not a scary monster but a harmless daimon wanting to communicate with me. Those who had seen Nareas in his three-torsoed form, my adorable black Labrador retriever shift into Cerberus, and all the spiders disperse from under Arachne's muumuu were split into two groups: those who saw with their own eyes the ancient pantheon lived anew in the temple of these mountains and those who also saw and decided they didn't want to get *that* up close and personal with their gods.

From an objective point of view, the latter made more sense. Faith was easier if you didn't have to know just how dangerous your deities were.

I had grown up with stories about the former mythological beings, but I hadn't known they were real—or that I'd come from the very real oracles of Delphi, likely a descendant of Dione and likely Zeus, and a harpy somewhere in there. I was brand new to gods and monsters too.

We started the whole ceremony again. I faked my way through the first three petitioners. The fourth was a young woman in a white chiton, with her midnight hair in long dreads pulled back from her dark brown face. Her high cheekbones and jawline seemed a little too sharp, like someone who didn't eat enough. Even slightly hidden in the loose fabric, her body showed signs of malnourishment.

The near starvation turned my stomach. I heaved an inward sigh. Even in the time of miracles and magic pulsing on every street, poverty and homelessness still existed.

The petitioner had done the purification rituals, wearing the garments the harpies posted gave her. Her thin fingers pulled at the material of her chiton. Her gaze pinged pillar to pillar, no doubt scanning for more monsters.

How did she come so far? The temple was in the mountains.

Eyes with copper irises sighted me the way someone takes aim at a target. She lifted her chin. In that moment she became as elegant and regal as The Twelve, despite her situation. "I want to dedicate myself to Athena and build her a temple, where women can devote themselves to serve her. Who do I see about that?"

Arachne's hand flew to her mouth, her olive skin blanching. The elderly woman murmured something and slipped away, skittering on spider legs to the back.

I faced the petitioner. Building of temples traditionally had been commissioned by politicians and the wealthy. This temple had been magically transferred from Olympus itself when these mountains were named the Olympics. The mention of the home of the gods gave them a power boost, so they put a temple here as kind of a lightning rod. At least, that's what Nicky told me. From my further research, I'd learned the temple also syphoned the awe the mountains inspired to Olympus. I had no idea how it worked or if it was ethical because the Olympians didn't create these mountains, but I wasn't the one benefitting from it.

I just worked here.

"I am but a simple servant of the gods myself with no authority to build or commission another a temple," I said spreading my hands. It was the truth, but I wasn't a fervent worshipper like this woman.

Her face fell, copper gaze lowering to her hands. "Oh."

The one word made my heart sink. How many times had I made that same face and felt that same rejection when I tried applying for waitressing gigs when I was sixteen and pregnant?

Arachne returned from the back. Her eyes were red and puffy, but I didn't see any tears. "This is a temple for all the gods, including Athena. You may pray to her for the wisdom to fund the building of a temple to her while you're here. However, a shrine at home is where you can begin. Do you know how to seek her in the traditional way?"

Hot shame pricked my skin. I should've guided the woman instead of telling her the equivalent of there's nothing I could do for her. My lack of faith in leaning on someone else sometimes failed to see the use of it for other people.

The woman shook her head. "All I know is what's on the internet, but I feel here." She pressed her hand on her heart. "And I know here." She touched her forehead. "Women desperately need her strength and wisdom right now. We're losing everything."

She had suffered much in her life, as many do. Unseen and unheard, she wanted a voice and the backing of someone much more powerful than she was. A goddess, a well-known goddess would give her the voice she needed.

Three squares and a roof over her head wouldn't hurt either.

"Would you like to serve this temple until you find a way to commission one for Athena?"

It was a shot in the dark.

"Well, I..." Her eyes darted between me and Arachne. The latter nodded and smiled her encouragement.

I know it would cost Arachne emotionally to have a devotee to Athena around, but she seemed on board with helping this woman out. Her kindness knew few bounds.

"Um, it would be hard for me to get here from Olympia on a regular basis. I hitched my way here today. Lucked out and found another devotee to Athena." She licked her lips. "How often would I need to come out?"

"If you would like to train with us to be a priestess of Athena, you would have to devote your entire life to the goddess," Arachne replied. I'm so glad the elderly woman caught on to where I was going.

"That would mean living with us." I almost said in the temple, but this place was too isolated. Also, I didn't want any of the gods with bad raps getting ideas. Hermes said many changed their modus operandi when it came to women, but I knew too many stories.

A smile brightened the woman's whole face, revealing she was quite beautiful. Her eyes wet with happy tears. "Okay."

"What's your name?"

She pinched her lips and crossed her arms.

Arachne and I exchanged a glance. Having many aliases, myself, I understood not wanting to give a fake name to representatives of the gods but at the same time not wanting to give away a real name and chance getting caught for something done in the past.

"We won't tell anyone your real name."

"It's not that," she said, sighing loudly and shaking her head. "I —I just don't like it. My parents thought it was cute. My dad was Greek, and mom, she liked the brand name. Everyone in school called me sneaker or kicks or shouted slogans at me."

"Nike?" I guessed.

"Nike Nora Smith." She sighed again and threw up her hands. "See why I hate it?"

"Nike is a goddess of victory and shared a temple with Athena in the acropolis because she was considered an aspect of Athena by some. This is a good name," Arachne said, grinning ear to ear. Sadness lingered in her eyes, but she seemed to be open to the idea of temples to her enemy.

Nike Nora Smith wrung her hands. "All the same—can you call me Nora outside the temple, please? That's what I like to go by."

It was a different situation, but with Luke, he protested the name we gave him since he was able to speak up for himself. For my son, he was assigned female at birth and didn't want the feminine name. I always went with the names he chose for himself—teasing him with Lukie now and then because I thought it was cute, but never dead-named him.

A name was a gift, but a gift was only a gift if the person wanted it. Otherwise, you were burdening someone with something they didn't want, to make yourself happy.

"We can call you Nora all the time, if you wish."

"Athena won't be displeased?" Her eyes brightened, but she bit her lower lip.

Arachne shook her head. "From someone who knew her well, Athena isn't a petty goddess. She understands your reasons, I'm sure. I will take you to the back and teach you a supplication ritual. We'll get your belongings later."

Nora took Arachne in. *All* of her. Her eyes widened. "Oh, you're..."

"Arachne," the elderly woman offered, lips quivering with barely contained emotion.

It had to be painful to see someone recall your story in real time. It might not be correct, but what happened between Arachne and Athena wasn't any less awful than the story.

I had to give it to Nora. She turned to me and asked, "And you're?"

I gave her a grateful smile and held out my hand. "Lydia Kourakos, Oracle to the Gods."

CHAPTER

FIVE

T he rest of the petitioners who came through got pre-oracle gift-types of predictions. I was glad that I gravitated toward divination and learned a long time ago how to read people to know what they want.

The sun hung low on the horizon beyond the temple walls when an argument broke out outside. A deep voice raised above the dual voices of the harpies.

"Let's see what's happening, Spot." I stood and lifted the chiton so the hem wouldn't drag through the stinky water in the ravine.

In his black lab guise, Cerberus trotted next to me past statues and columns down a set of marble stairs to a foyer.

A young man and an older man, both dressed in off-the-rack suits with a leather messenger bag slung over the shoulder argued with the harpies.

"You are not of this world, foul creature," the balding white-haired man shouted in a harpy's face.

She calmly placed her arms between herself and the assailant. "I need you to leave. This sanctuary is private property."

The harpies were here for security, but they didn't like to lay hands on mundanes. Nicky said it was bad press. The protocol was to let the Christian fanatics shout away until they laid hands on someone. It made the zealots appear as brainwashed and sometimes as unstable as they truly were and showed that we were reasonable and calm. No need to fight over what's right when we knew the Olympians existed.

Their god hadn't made an appearance. Hermes said he couldn't exist in this realm because the widespread belief of the Abrahamic religions and the demise of the regional pantheons gave their deity so much power, he'd ascended to something akin to pure magic and was no longer capable of crossing into this world let alone communicating the way most do. In other words, their god was overpowered and couldn't relate to us plebs anymore.

To me, ascension sounded awful. Whoever wanted to be like that was beyond me. Also, beyond the gods of Olympus, who Hermes said liked their flesh. Indeed, they did.

"Can't you see these women are the whores of Babylon. Minions of the devil, sent to turn the eyes of men from God," the younger man shouted to the remainder of the petitioners, ripping me from thoughts of godly flesh.

The man started flailing about wildly. Both harpies homed in on him, restraining the zealot. While they were busy, the old man rushed me.

Liquid sprayed from some sort of squirter, stinging my eyes. My nose ran, and I coughed uncontrollably.

Pepper spray.

Damn it.

Someone grabbed my arm. Vertigo set in. Noise muffled.

No, no, no!

I couldn't go into an oracle trance now.

~

I FOLLOWED *the priestess into a cave. It was cold and damp inside and smelled of must and something metallic. Copper, maybe?*

She promised that if I survived the test, I would be able to see the future. See how my brothers in the Resistance could oust the Italian soldiers occupying our country. We fought so hard against them, but the Nazis, the Bulgarians, and Italians all at once proved too much.

They carved up my country, taking this piece for one and that piece for the other. They made us toil and stole our food from our plates.

The jerks should've read their history books. This wasn't the first time someone invaded us for our resources, our hard work. We would win our land back. We always did.

"I will be able to read the thread for anything, not just have these dreams that come true?" I asked for the millionth time.

The priestess to the old gods glanced over her shoulder. "You will gain exact knowledge for the questions you ask."

We came to a pillar as tall as a mountain and pure black, yet gleaming, like crystalline waters of a lake at midnight. Vibrations resonated through my body, rattling my bones.

"Is this it? Seems like an electric motor is running inside it."

The priestess's gaze set on the pillar, she replied, "It holds great power. More power than any modern engine could emit."

I licked my lips. "This thing isn't going to electrocute me, will it?"

She swung her dark gaze in my direction. "If you do not accept the power of the oracle, the gate will devour you, body and soul."

Gooseflesh rose on my arms. I tried rubbing away the chill. I knew this would be dangerous. The priestess told me it would. Prayers to the saints hadn't worked. I needed the might of the old gods. I'd already seen the power it had given the priestess.

Chewing my bottom lip and rubbing my arms wasn't going to give me anything but brush burn and a swollen mouth. I had to act.

I reached for the pillar.

The woman blocked me. "One last thing. Among many other things, a door will appear in your mind. Don't open it."

"What happens if I do?"

She didn't answer right away. Instead, she took my measure with eyes that seemed to see me better than I knew myself. When she finally spoke, she said in a voice so calm, you'd think she was soothing a child. "You will unleash the primordial gods, the Titans, who existed before the Olympians. You will unleash their mighty fury unto the world."

The calm unnerved me, but only for so long. I had faced soldiers with deadly calm and lived.

"If I offered myself as a sacrifice, would they attack the Italian forces?"

She cut me a glare that made my blood freeze. "The Titans would annihilate mankind in retribution for their imprisonment."

I shuddered.

"If you don't heed my advice and open the door, know that you will die first before they slaughter everyone you love. Maybe the Titans will leave a piece of you to go to the Underworld. I doubt it, but joining your family and everyone you love in the afterlife is a lovely thought."

"Fine. Fine! I won't open the door."

The priestess stepped out of my way, giving me a wide berth.

I took a deep breath, stepped forward and touched the obsidian pillar.

Agony, white-hot and blinding, sliced through me. A scream tore from my lips. My eyes and nose ran. The taste of the coppery-sweet-salt of blood wetting my open mouth. A void swallowed the edges of my vision, threatening to drown me in darkness, until finally pulling me under.

SOMEONE TUCKED me into my own bed. A damp cloth cooled on my forehead. Cerberus's heads snored somewhere close. One nestled on my lap.

The click of Arachne's knitting needles alerted me to her presence and soothed me.

"How long was I out?"

A question asked often after prediction days.

The needles didn't stop as she lifted her gaze from her work. "Seven hours."

I nodded and grabbed a glass of water. "Everyone eat?"

"About two hours ago. I put Nora in a guest room. She went with Nicky to get her belongings."

Olympia was about two hours' drive south of Milagro Bay. I couldn't believe Nora had hitchhiked that far.

Western Washington was a temperate rain forest. Even when it wasn't pouring, there was a constant misty drizzle, or as Nicky called it "mizzle". No matter the season, the area remained damp and cool. A week or so each summer we got sun and heat.

The distance and weather would make for miserable hitchhiking. Nora was made of tough stuff, and her devotion to Athena was unwavering.

"Someone like her should be the Oracle, not a grifter like me."

The needles stopped the incessant clicking. Arachne turned to me fully. "There have been many Oracles who didn't go into a trance at all. They made up their predictions to suit their motives and those of the gods. Being the Oracle isn't an altruistic service like a charity. You're an employee of the Olympian marketing department, just as any holy person has been for their gods from time immemorial. Knowing how to tell people what they want to hear just makes you good at your job and good at making people able to go on with their day. Call it motivational speaking, if you will. Reading the threads?" She shrugged. "That's just what Clotho and her sisters have spun, foreseeing the future really doesn't serve anyone any good. Que sera sera."

"Whatever will be will be," I sang, grinning.

"Exactly."

I sighed. "There's one problem. Luke can't leave Milagro Bay if he can't control his oracle gift."

As much as I loved my boy staying with me, he had a job and a life in Seattle with Juan. Luke could work from home, but he was expected in the office occasionally for all-hands meetings. Also, Juan's commute would eventually put a strain on him and their relationship.

Arachne squeezed my hand. "No one knows if an oracle has control or not but the oracle. You should know that, Lydia."

Indeed. I'd fooled the Twelve.

"Do you know a way I could hitch a ride to Hades without Hermes?"

She frowned. "What do you want to do there?"

"My mother's shade is in Asphodel. I need to talk to her about Dione." I didn't want to talk to Apollonia at all. We didn't have the reunion I had hoped for, and to say I was disappointed in her for more reasons than abandoning me was an understatement. Also, the last time I saw my mother, her shade form flickered and faded like a hologram on a sci-fi show. However, she might be able to recall surviving Dione's test. I'd much rather learn from her how to survive than to owe Nareas a godhood.

Daimons weren't evil, but they weren't good either.

"There was a time I could bring you to Persephone myself or anywhere else in the multiverse you'd like to go. However, I made a mistake in a crossroads bar that got me in a heap of trouble with The Twelve. Caused a whole thing between the angels and Olympia. Zeus said I'm no longer welcome to roam the realms. Nicky will have to take you."

I quirked an eyebrow. "Did you eat an angel?"

"No." Arachne grinned, resuming her knitting. "Well, not directly. I wrapped the jerk wad in spider silk and fed my children."

"Why?"

"A long time ago, the fae and the angels fought. The angels won. That wasn't good enough for this one. The asshat claimed a fae he had with him at the hotel was a prisoner of war. You don't keep a prisoner of war chained to you like a pet."

My hand flew to my mouth. "What happened to the fae?"

"She passed away."

"Oh no! That wasn't the ending I expected."

She chuckled. "Oh, that was recently. The fae lived a full life, albeit short for a high fae, before that happened. After we watched my children devour her angelic jailor, she didn't want to go back to faerie. Too many bad memories from the war. Before I was called to Olympus, I brought her to my motel to live with me. When I got the call from Hermes to appear before The Twelve, I asked for a few days to hide the fae. Witches took her in, believing she was a halfling witch without a coven. I may have helped them with that belief." Arachne winked.

"Such a do-gooder."

She paused her knitting to wave the notion off. "Before she passed, she had a daughter. You've met her, I think." Arachne sighed a happy sigh. "That Rhiannon has really done a lot for herself. I see her mother in her eyes. I wonder if she knows she's a halfling, not just one-sixteenth brownie."

'd tried every avenue available to me researching how Oracles accessed their gift and what the gate had to do with it. My predecessors said nothing. Maybe it was always a trick. A lie so that they would open the gates. There was only one way left to find out, and that was asking Nicky to take me to the Underworld. She'd flat out refused before I could finish explaining.

I followed her from the dining room to the kitchen. "The thing is, if you don't take me to the Underworld, I'll not only have my gift to worry about but Nareas blabbing to the gods or anyone else who will listen that I don't know what I'm doing."

"I said *no*," Nicky slammed her coffee mug on the counter with enough force for it to shatter. Coffee and shards of ceramic spilled everywhere. She burst into sobs.

I rushed to her side, shooing her away from the mess. "Let me help. It's my fault. I insisted, not thinking about how much I'd upset you."

"Sorry," she said, breathing heavily into her palms covering her face. The handle of the mug was still attached to her finger. "I can't."

"It's okay." I tentatively picked up the broken pieces, careful not to cut myself. "I shouldn't have pushed. Hermes will be back." *Eventually.*

"Lucinda might do it. She is a general of Persephone's army after all. Let me give her a call and ask." Nicky left the room without waiting for my response.

I finished cleaning up the mess, hoping that I'd be able to repair our relationship as easily when I got back. After I finished cleaning, I went upstairs shortly after. There was something I wanted to bring along if Lucinda said yes.

AN HOUR LATER, a siren landed in my backyard.

Lucinda wore nothing but her armor. Colorful feathers on her body. Harpies were pretty with their golden wings and feathers, but sirens were ... something else. Looking at one was like looking at a diamond chandelier and wearing a silk gown the chandelier gave you at once.

I gawked at her for much longer than politeness dictated.

"Ready?" She signaled, sparing me from her voice.

I nodded, unable to speak but for entirely different reasons.

Cerberus loped beside me, nudging my hand. He was the three-headed beast, not the black Lab guise.

Lucinda's arms enveloped my waist. Something gold and shiny peeked from between her fingers of her clenched fist. The next thing I knew we were airborne, flying through the "Tron" space between universes with Cerberus galloping right below her feet.

My skin felt stretched like a rubber band pulled to capacity. Then that band snapped, and we were in front of what I recognized as the obsidian palace of Persephone. Two more sirens, who stood guard at the entrance, greeted us with nods and hand signals. That was for my benefit. Nicky told me they could communicate with each other.

Persephone herself stepped out of doors that stretched two

stories high. She smiled, extending her hands. "I hoped you'd be back, Lydia."

It was nice to receive such a welcome. I doubted Persephone greeted all her guests at the door. However, she didn't invite me in.

"I need to see my mother."

Persephone offered me her arm. "Shall we?"

Arms linked, we headed away from the castle. Lucinda stayed behind, as if she'd already been told what to do when she arrived. We followed a glittering road for a while before coming onto a field.

Persephone raised her free hand. Her chest glowed magenta right where her sternum should be.

Within moments, my mother appeared, or at least the shade of what was left of her arrived. Apollonia's eyes were black pits, lacking sclerae, irises, or pupils.

"You look like my mother, but you are not," she said.

I glanced at Persephone.

She whispered in my ear, "A shattered shade like your mother is unable to recall much after her death."

A shard, sharp and jagged as the pieces of Nicky's broken mug, pierced my chest. No wonder my stepmother didn't want to see her late wife. It would be like visiting someone with advanced dementia or late-stage Alzheimer's.

"I'm a relative." I didn't want to go through the lackluster mother daughter reunion again.

The shade nodded but made no comment.

"Apollonia, did Dione teach you how to use your oracle gifts?"

She shook her head. "The bitch made me hurt to learn how. Matrix and medieval shit all wrapped in one. Downloaded all the knowledge in my brain by touching the magic stone."

"Did you have to place your palms on the gates of Tartarus to learn?"

Apollonia picked at her fingers. "No, it's in Delphi, mortal realm Greece. The cave of the first oracle, which is surprise, surprise, Dione."

The cave in Delphi could've led to Hades and the gates of Tartarus. There was a cave under the lake in Colorado which led to Hades. The Titans Echidna and Typhon showed me that much.

"Did you open the door?"

Apollonia stopped picking her fingers and grinned. Looking up at me with her horror movie eyes, she replied in a teasing tone, "Not that time."

Persephone drew in a sharp breath. She opened her mouth as if to speak.

I squeezed her hand. We had to be careful, or Apollonia might blip out on us.

"Oh?" I said. "I didn't know anyone could."

"How do you think Typhon got out?" Her brows furrowed. "I couldn't keep it open for the rest."

Apollonia began to flicker. "No. I was helping! Why did they?"

"That's enough," Persephone commanded, her chest glowing as she spoke.

My mother waved and walked away.

"WHAT IS this door you spoke of?" the queen of Hades asked.

We sat in what she called her morning room, having tea. Apparently, talking about this in Asphodel wasn't safe. I didn't know why, but I believed Persephone.

I related Nareas's appearance and what I'd dreamt of a past oracle.

"I wonder," Persephone began, taking a sip of her tea before continuing, "if my father would appreciate knowing these machinations or if he's behind them."

"What?"

"What better way to elevate Olympus than to release an old enemy unto the mortal realm and then defeat them?"

I shook my head. "I'm not following."

"The Olympians defeated the Titans and locked them away in Tartarus when the Titans were at the height of their power. The Titans are less spoken of, less well known by the mortals as gods. They're known as the losers of the Titanomachy, not worshiped or even sung about like the gods. This would weaken them. I know I grew in power as I was popularized in the modern era."

Persephone had made it into three blockbusters, in the late 1990s and early 2000s, thanks to the Wachowski sisters' Matrix movies. The Olympians made it into too many modern books, comics, and movies to count. Ask anyone to name an Olympian and a name would roll off their tongue. Titans would take more time.

"If that's true and another Titanomachy occurs, mund—mortals will die."

The beautiful goddess casted a dark glance at a faraway place I couldn't see with my human eyes. "I don't want my kingdom to grow with victims of war just so my father can gain power."

She squeezed my hand.

Our surroundings swirled, like oil dropped on a wet painted canvas. When the colors solidified into shapes, we were standing before the obsidian pillar I'd seen in my vision.

Must be nice to be a god.

My ancestor had the description right. The obsidian hummed with power like the vibrations of an engine.

"If the vision and your mother's assessment were correct, all you need to do is press your hands against the obsidian." She gave me a warning look that sent frissons down my spine. "Don't open the door."

"Dying to let the Titans out wasn't on my to-do list today," I muttered under my breath as I approached the pillar with my hands outstretched.

I hesitated just a breath away from touching the stone. "If Dione told my mother and two of my ancestors not to open the door, and Echidna met my mother and convinced her separately to open it to get Typhon out, who got Echidna out?"

"Good question," Persephone replied. "Revealing how to use your oracle powers, might help you read the weave of the past."

I turned. "What happens if it was Zeus?"

Her face darkened. "Then my husband and I confront him. If Olympus is behind his actions..."

"War?"

Her face was colder than I'd ever seen it. "I will not have mortals dying over my father's ambitions."

Hermes would have to pick sides in such a war. All the gods would. It could tear up the pantheon, and things might end up like they did for the fae. I knew little about the Fae Wars other than they were almost wiped out of existence by the angels. That's what happened when two powerful forces collided. Nobody won.

"What if it wasn't Zeus?"

"Then my father will punish who did. Either way, you need to learn how to use your powers."

She was right. If a god was trying to create a new Titanomachy to garner belief, then reading the weave of the past and future would be helpful in stopping it from happening.

Closing my eyes, I pressed my palms against the pillar. I expected a jolt or to feel pulled apart like my ancestors. Instead, the obsidian absorbed me.

Dark, warm liquid surrounded me. I twisted and turned, trying to find the surface to escape my watery death to no avail. Unable to find a source of light to swim toward, I floated. And floated.

My lungs burned. Part of me wanted to relent to the instinct to inhale.

There!

In the distance, a pinprick of light appeared. I gathered what little strength I could muster to swim toward the dot. The pinprick grew. My arms and legs ached with effort. Spots danced before my eyes. I wasn't going to make it.

A current formed in the erstwhile motionless liquid, sweeping me toward the light.

CHAPTER

SEVEN

Air rushed into my lungs as I burst through a barrier, reviving me. I gulped as much as I could before I felt the pull of gravity. Realizing I was no longer suspended by liquid, my stomach bottomed out.

As I fell to my death, a sparkling city of lights and architecture like I've never seen before spread before me. Silver crafts zipped through the air around the buildings, all too distant to catch a falling middle-aged mom.

If my demise wasn't strange enough, a silver dildo the size of a small sedan flew by, reversed and then matched my speed of freefall. I was plummeting to my death neck and neck with the giant silver penis.

Despite my fear, I cackled.

Who will finish first?

I was falling to my death, but I hadn't lost my sense of humor.

Something shot out of the ... er ... tip of the craft. Suddenly, I was entangled in netting, being hauled toward the head. The hole the net hung from dilated until it was big enough to accommodate my body.

Once I and the tangled mess of netting slid inside the silver, sedan-sized, dildo, the hole contracted.

The pungent, cloying odor of seafood smacked my nostrils.

Two people with gills on their necks like the nymph I'd met in Hermes's bathroom in the palace on Olympus. Unlike his sister, these people didn't have legs. Instead, they walked on furcated fishtails.

"Well, at least it's not snakes."

The two exchanged a glance. One lifted an eyebrow, and the other one shrugged.

Ohhhh. I'd spoken in English.

They were melusina or as my grandfather called them, "sirena bicauda." Unlike the feathered sirens of Persephone's army, they were of Triton's ilk. They were also known as merfolk in a modern context. These two didn't have mammalian breasts, and looked built to carry very big things, so I guess they'd be mermen, but I wasn't going to assume their gender. They were magical beings with fishtails for legs. That's all I needed to know.

"Let me guess. You want to be part of my world?" I asked in Greek. The joke must have been lost in translation because they both wrinkled their nose.

"No. The king wishes to see you. Please, sit until we arrive at the palace."

Great. I wasn't in just any giant penis flown by melusinas, I was in Poseidon's penis.

All the gods seemed to want a piece of the Oracle. Lucky me. Too bad Persephone was the only one who tried to help me learn how to use my gift.

They strapped me into a seat that smelled a lot like sardines and returned to wherever they were before. Wonderful hosts, these Atlanteans.

The walls were semitransparent, enabling me to see above and below as well as side to side. The city was truly a wonder, far more advanced than anything on Earth, Olympus, Hades, or Miriam's faerie.

It was kinda neat that I got to see so many worlds. It would be even more awesome if I'd come as a *visitor* instead of a prisoner. I was getting real sick of gods pushing me here and there. Someday I might find a way to put my foot down and refuse to go. It would be nice to have the power to demand they come to me with their problems.

The ship flew over a city that seemed to be a domed island surrounded by water.

The largest building looked more like a Chihuly exhibit with colorful glass spires and fanciful twists and turns than a place where a king lived let alone functioned as ruler. Taking the whole thing in, the palace reminded me of a coral reef. I suppose that's the impression the architect meant to give since Poseidon ruled the seas.

"Wow."

The two merfolk murmured their agreement.

More phallic looking ships docked in holes of the rose-colored anemones' portion of the coral reef palace.

I covered my mouth in a failed attempt to stifle a giggle. Yes, I was over forty, but I had the sense of humor of a sixteen-year-old.

"What is so funny?"

I gestured to the pink anemone. "Come on. I can't be the only one who noticed this."

"It is the Imperial Dock of the Mighty Eel Navy. We're much more advanced than any mortal world has ever conceived—why are you laughing?"

I cleared my throat and gathered my composure as best as possible, which wasn't very well at all. "This vessel represents an eel?"

The two merfolk nodded in affirmation. One regarded me as if I were not quite all there. The other simply seemed to believe I was purposefully mocking them—which I kinda was. The more offended of the two said, "The representation of an eel is clear by the vessel's shape. How can you not see these are eels entering the orifices of an anemone?" He gestured outside.

I chose to look at them instead of following the gesture. The ostensible eels looked like dildos to me, and I couldn't unsee it. I shook my head, biting my lip.

"Perhaps she hasn't ever seen an eel?" the other suggested.

"I have not," I admitted—*at least not in person.* "The vessels have the appearance of something I've only seen ... on land. It's a very funny creature."

This confession seemed to mollify the offended one of the two. They went about their business of docking in the port.

The "Mighty Eel Navy" wasn't Poseidon's only phallic symbol poorly disguised as something else. The grand columns holding up the ceiling of the shiny glass palace were also "eels". Questionable dolphin columns interspersed between the eels made me glad that at least the seahorses were seahorses—I hoped.

I needed to recall all I knew about Poseidon. I knew he fought Athena for control of Athens. That he had a wife, Amphitrite. She wasn't too keen on marrying him in the first place. She ran to Atlas, but Poseidon got a dolphin to woo her for him or something like that. None of that knowledge would help me now.

Instead of a throne room, the merfolk led me down narrower and narrower passageways into what seemed to be a private quarter since it was furnished less like an official palace visitor's room and more like a den in a home—a very fancy home.

Persephone had taken me into a similar type of room in her Underworld palace. Also, Hermes took me to his personal quarters in the Olympian palace, and it had the same appeal. Hera and Apollo sought me out there. Excepting Zeus and most of his lot, it seemed even gods preferred their living spaces than dealing with the pomp and circumstance of their own throne rooms.

Poseidon, or I assumed the burly man with silver hair and beard sitting with a book by a fireplace was Poseidon, peered up from his leatherbound book with eyes the aquamarine of the sea at a Caribbean coastline. His skin was the darker olive complexion shared by Hermes, Zeus, Persephone, and me. The contrast of silver hair, eyes, and skin would make him a striking figure alone, but this god also had a Greek nose, strong cheekbones, and the build of a sailor, grizzled and hardened by years working at sea.

What struck me most wasn't Poseidon's looks, but the deep sorrow in his light eyes. He rose.

"Thank you, seamen."

I blinked, but when the merfolk left, I understood my brain misspelled what he'd said.

"Please, make yourself at home. Have a seat wherever you'd like," he offered as if this was any den of any home, not the king of the sea in his palace.

I sat on a loveseat with pretty, silver brocade fabric. Poseidon positioned himself next to me. He had a warm and fatherly air about him, like my grandfather. The god was much older than my grandfather had been when he passed, but the god's face bore far fewer lines.

He laid a comforting hand on my shoulder. "You have nothing to worry about. As long as you're in my domain, you're safe, Lydia Kourakos."

I managed a smile. Gods didn't make promises lightly.

"I didn't know your mother, but I'd like to offer my condolences."

"Thank you, but I didn't know her either. No condolences necessary."

He sighed. "A rule my brother insisted. There is no reason why an oracle can't be a mother and serve the gods. Zeus has always been jealous of his priestesses' time. What I can't figure out is why he killed Thetis."

My heart lurched in my chest. "What?" Why would Zeus have killed Thetis? She kidnapped me from Olympus, but I assumed she had her own designs.

"I can't understand why he killed Thetis. We'd both loved her ... once upon a time." A tear slid from his eye, rolling down his cheek.

I doubted it was "once" for Poseidon. Perhaps that was why he saw me privately. The gods, like my ex, were always carrying on with some side piece. Seemed the nymph had meant a lot more to this god than a casual affair.

"I'm sorry for your loss," I said and meant it.

He flashed a rueful smile, there and gone. "I lost Thetis a long time ago, back when power and maintaining rule of my domain mattered to me more than love."

"Hindsight is—" I paused. The phrase didn't translate to Greek well.

"Hindsight is twenty-twenty?" he offered in English, a grin forming on his lips.

"Yes." I grinned back, cheeks flooding with heat. What was wrong with me? I wasn't a teenager, and he was a very married god. Not to mention, Hermes and I were kind of a thing. Okay. Definitely a thing. A thing we hadn't sealed the deal on, but still.

"I would have invited you to Atlantis instead of bringing you here by dubious means, but as I've said before, Zeus is jealous of his servants, and I am going to ask you to do something that may cause discord between my realm and Olympus."

"Ask ... not demand?"

He shook his head. "A gift freely offered is sweeter than all the stolen goods of the realms."

Okay. It seemed Poseidon was working a little too hard to charm me. I made sure to have my mental guards up and watched his face for signs he'd been digging. I saw none.

"I can't take you for long, so I'll ask now. Will you read the threads for me, Oracle?"

I couldn't admit to Poseidon that I didn't know how to access my oracular gift on demand and properly read the threads. That would mean my predictions were random threads and unreliable.

"I can try."

The king of the sea nodded, then produced a metal flask with a triton carved on the side. "Drink this. It will help induce the state you need to be in for a prediction."

I took the flask and stared at it. "What did you want to know?"

"It's best I ask while you are in your oracle state. I like my secrets held close." He gave me a meaningful look.

He knew. He knew I didn't have full access to my abilities. Thetis must've figured it out and told him before she died. Which lead me to wonder if Zeus killed her or if he wanted to cover his tracks because he wanted to open the gates to Tartarus.

I took a deep breath. If I refused, everyone who knew anything had last seen me go to Persephone. I'd been nowhere near water when I slipped through the gate into Atlantis. My death couldn't be traced back to Poseidon. Is this how my mother actually died? Poseidon stepping in on Zeus's plans.

"Surely the daughter of Apollonia knows a god is bound to his word."

He'd said no harm would come to me.

I uncapped the flask and sniffed the contents. "Seawater? I can't drink tha..." The flask fell from my hand, spilling onto the floor.

CHAPTER

EIGHT

I didn't quite go under as usual, I was aware of Poseidon and that I was speaking, but I felt as if "Lydia" was set aside to watch another person who took the helm of my body.

The king of Atlantis asked questions. She answered in the same archaic Greek as the Titans had spoken in. I could understand very little of the actual words but could understand intention. She felt like part of me, a part that had been locked behind a door my whole life. A fractured part like a numb limb. Except the limb moved and spoke. The helplessness, the lack of control of an essential part of me somehow felt worse than being completely unaware of what I was doing and saying.

Anger, hot and bright flaring but also remote. I seethed, after screaming inside with nothing coming out of my mouth.

I watched Poseidon's lip quiver. Tears formed rivulets down his cheek, darkening his silver beard.

Even though his demand upon me put me in this infuriating situation, I couldn't blame him for wanting to know. Poseidon had loved Thetis before the most countries of the modern mundane world existed, before the Romans conquered most of Europe.

If Carlo had treated me better, I'd be distraught over my twenty-year marriage ending. Maybe I was. Since Dione walked through my shop's door, I hadn't had the time to even consider let alone process my feelings. The part of me who had loved Carlo, the younger me who had thought he was the sun, moon, and stars, mourned with Poseidon. That part reached for his hand, as I would any client in distress and squeezed.

The part of me who was The Oracle spoke on dispassionately.

The king observed my hand and my face. His thick silver eyebrows knitted together.

Yes. I'm in here. I care, even if she doesn't.

He squeezed my hand back.

The small acknowledgement, the connection of one hurting soul consoling another, lifted some of my frustration and anger. I wasn't just a tool to him, but a person. It warmed me that Hermes and Persephone weren't the only gods who cared. The rest on Olympus seemed distant, time eroding sentiment and empathy.

Perhaps that wasn't a fair assessment. I'd only spoken directly to Zeus, Apollo, and Hera. Hera and Zeus seemed like politicians, cold and aloof, plotting their next machinations. Apollo a bored heir with all the time to pursue his hobbies, no wonder he was a patron god of the arts.

The part of me that was the oracle finished her prophecy, drawing away and disappearing to wherever in my psyche she lived.

I gasped for air as if I remembered breathing was a thing I had to do.

Poseidon tightened his grip and clutched my shoulder with his free hand. "It's okay. Take your time."

I nodded, exhaustion dragging at the corners of my consciousness.

"Thank you for your assistance. I—I didn't know the toll it takes on you. I'll have my seamen take you to a room where you can recover."

Part of me wanted to argue, the part that knew people waited for me, but I could barely keep my eyes open.

Poseidon gave me one last look before leaving the room.

I lay back in the chair, not fighting the growing weight on my eyelids.

~

I woke in a bed fit for a queen, or a goddess, with silky, pale pink sheets and a champagne comforter, knowing exactly where I was and what had happened.

A black-haired woman with a streak of silver framing her face stood at the edge of the bed. She wore a golden crab claw tiara and a floor length belted chiton, also decorated with crab claws. Her dark eyes narrowed on me, assessing. Her crown could mean she was Amphitrite, but I wouldn't assume so until she told me that.

She frowned. "I thought the Oracle had to be young."

I rubbed my eyes and stretched. She didn't ask a question, nor did she greet me, so I didn't feel compelled to respond.

"What did you tell him?"

I cocked my head to the side. "You'll have to be more specific. I'm an old oracle, you see, and I tell a lot of hims a lot of things."

"Don't be obtuse. You know I meant my husband."

Ah, so it was Amphitrite.

"I don't recall."

"He wanted a reason to war with Zeus over that naiad. Did you give it to him?"

"I don't think so. I also don't think he's going to war with his brother. There are more important things to worry about."

"Oh, Dione suddenly decided to free her family after a few thousand years of captivity?" She sniffed. "Zeus is looking for his glory days and blaming an old flame for the trouble he's causing, as usual."

Persephone, Poseidon, and now Amphitrite all expressed they

believed Zeus was behind it all. I wasn't so sure. He certainly seemed interested in discovering what Typhon and Echidna were up to. Someone who planned the chaos wouldn't care, but I kept all these thoughts to myself. Amphitrite wouldn't get anything out of me other than what she demanded.

I lifted the covers from my legs, swinging my feet over the side of the bed. Someone had left my shoes on the floor right next to the frame. The thoughtfulness touched me.

Amphitrite eyed me as I slipped on my sandals. "You have the look of an Olympian, but so do many of your line. Even now, after the treaties with the angels. The question is how far back or if you're a child of his. Who was he?"

"I don't know." I didn't think I looked like the Olympians. I was attractive but not godly attractive. I was also a middle-aged woman. We weren't really the media beauty standard on Earth.

"Why don't you read the threads of the past and find out?"

I shrugged.

"Don't you want to know?

"Not really."

Who my father was didn't matter. He didn't raise me and didn't get to know me before. I didn't care to get to know him now in my forties. I wasn't heir to anything and wasn't about to inherit anything other than whatever supernatural problems came with whatever deity or supernatural got busy with Apollonia over forty years ago.

"It could play to your advantage. I bet it's one of the brothers."

My stomach felt queasy. I groaned. I didn't want to be secretly one of their kids. I knew it was different among gods. Hades was Persephone's uncle etc. However, I'd been raised mundane and the thought of being related to someone I kissed with tongue, among other things, didn't sit well.

"They know their ilk. You didn't find it odd that a god offered his private chambers to you?"

I sighed. "Look, I've made it forty-four years without knowing. I simply don't care."

"Family is everything."

"Not every family," I replied over my shoulder. My grandparents raised me. I didn't need to know my father.

Amphitrite gripped my arm. "You don't walk away from a queen in her domain."

I looked at her hand. Every single ounce of me was sick and tired of beings more powerful than I was dragging me this way and that. I didn't care anymore about what they wanted and how they thought I should act. I had my own life, my own family, and my own desires. I wasn't some vessel for them to pass around for their objectives.

I should've lost my shit on Poseidon for dragging me here. I should have lost it on Zeus. I should have, and maybe I would in the future, but neither had *laid hands* on me.

"As far as I know, I serve Olympus and Olympians, not Atlantis. I'm not your subject, Amphitrite. I can walk away from you any time I wish. Let go."

We stared at each other. Part of me wished I could zap her, but mostly I wanted my words and my will to be my weapon.

Amphitrite let go, taking a step back.

Knocking thundered at the door.

"My queen! Atlantis is under siege!"

I recognized the seaman's voice as one of the two who fished me from midair with their flying dildo, eel, whatever.

"I'll be right there," she called and then turned to me, accusation sparking in her eyes. "Why didn't you tell my husband this was coming?"

First off, no oracle could see everything all the time, but I wasn't going to tell her that. "He didn't ask for the future. I only see what is asked of me."

At least, my excuse sounded true. I saw a lot more—things I didn't know I wanted to see. I don't know why I didn't see the past this time. I didn't know how any of my powers worked. Thanks to Poseidon, I wouldn't know until I got back.

Amphitrite eyed me. "You don't know how to use your gift. It just flows through you, doesn't it?"

I clamped my mouth shut.

Her features shifted into a look of pity. "Your secret is safe with me. I've always suspected that's how the oracle gift worked. Zeus will use you until you are of no use. Don't let him or any Olympians know. They will lose the modicum of respect they have for the oracles and treat them like vessels."

They already did. Still, I said nothing. I didn't know Amphitrite, but I tended to not trust people who were hot and cold with me in the same conversation.

The door rumbled again. A muffled shout came from outside, "The city is under siege, your majesty."

"Stay here until it is safe." she warned as she left.

CHAPTER

NINE

Tired of being told where to go and what to do, I decided I wasn't staying to see how the battle turned out. Ear to the door, I listened to Amphitrite and the seamen march away. Then I listened for any evidence of a seaman standing guard.

After listening to not so much as a breath from the other side, I tried the handle. To my surprise, the knob turned, and the door swung open. Cautiously, I peered outside, finding the well-lit corridor devoid of any presence.

Okay. Left or right?

Deciding on left, I dashed down a lavish marble floor. A mosaic of oceanic life surrounding Atlantis covered the walls. Doors to other rooms were indicated by recesses that looked like underwater caves. I tried a few. None budged.

The thought that I would never get out this way popped up again and again. I smacked it with a hammer. There was no time for doubt.

The hallway forked. In one direction, light and commotion signaled people and potential trouble. The other way led to silence and eerie darkness. Reasoning where there was noise, there were exits, I headed toward the light.

I missed Cerberus, Arachne, Nicky, my boys, and Hermes. The thought of Hermes reminded me I had a way out. I reached into my bra and pulled out the coin Hermes gave me in case I needed him while he was in Olympus. There had to be an intersection in Atlantis, and when I found it, I had my golden ticket home.

SLINKING off to a dark hallway sounded like a much better idea after reaching the source of the commotion.

An entire wall of the palace crumbled under the weight of a grayish purple tentacle bigger than Typhon's entire body, and that dude was massive. Seamen flew silver "eels" and "dolphins." The crafts shot laser beams at the tentacle.

Speaking of Typhon, or as I called him, Brad, the Titan stood at least three stories high. Animal heads lined his left and right shoulders and, in the middle, a giant nightmare head larger than the rest sat. The monstrous heads shrieked, roared, cawed, barked, and hissed simultaneously as my erstwhile kidnapper faced Poseidon.

The mighty King of Atlantis and God of the Sea raised his famed trident. Brad wielded a sickle-like sword.

If that wasn't enough of a cluster fork, my former bestie Jen, aka Echidna, showed up. Or at least her snake children had invaded the palace.

I shrieked as two wrapped around each of my legs.

"Oh, shit no," I shouted while hiking up my skirt to reach the sheath of the knife my grandparents gave me. It was awkward as heck and nothing like the movies. I kicked off a snake on one leg while I struggled to free my "knife" that was almost the length of my thigh.

Finally, I freed the knife. The blade stretched the length of my forearm with a hook toward the tip. No wonder I couldn't free it quickly! I immediately put it to use on the snake. The thing hissed a warning and then turned to stone.

It dawned on me that the knife was no knife, but harpe—*the* harpe. The blade Perseus had used to kill Medusa. Her shed blood must've imbued harpe with the power to turn flesh into stone like Medusa's stare.

Jen rushed at me. In halting English, she said, "Stop. No move. I protect key. Come with me." She beckoned with one of her monstrous appendages.

The snakes were meant to keep me alive so she could use me to open the door to Tartarus. I raised my knife-sword and replied in Greek, "Don't step any closer."

More of the building collapsed as a second tentacle smashed its way through. Phallic eel and dolphin vessels careened from the blow like bowling pins struck in midair. Explosions followed as some of the vessels crashed.

Atlantis was losing against a Titan even bigger than Brad.

Debris and dust exploded nearby, cutting me off. A third tentacle struck the ground. Thrown off-balance by the quake that followed, I teetered forward, flailing my arms—including the one holding the harpe.

Jen lunged at the same time. My hand came inches from her shoulder. Harpe sliced her arm clean off. Stone veins ran from where the blade cut. The severed arm turned to rock. Jen wailed and hissed.

"I'm sorry," I cried in Greek, righting myself. The full weight of what I'd done, slicing as deep as the blade. I hadn't meant to harm her.

She had no time to respond before a writhing tentacle crashed into us. Everything slowed as Jen and I sailed through the air at least five feet off the ground.

I screamed as we hurtled through the air, terrified for both my life and hers.

Stone spread until Jen was no longer flesh and blood. The last thing I saw was Jen's petrified face.

TEN

I don't know how long I was unconscious before my eyes fluttered open. My brain felt like it had played pinball in my skull and lost. Every single part of my body cried out in some sort of hurt.

The cacophony of battle still raged on around me but distant and muffled, ringing in my ears drowning it out.

Next to me, Jen's stone head lay in pieces, her memorialized scream in shambles. The heads of the snakes on her body broken. Her bifurcated snake tale lower half was pulverized into shards and dust.

"All the king's horses and all the king's men." There was no putting Humpty Dumpty back together again. The word irrevocable rang in my head louder than the din in my ears.

I had done an irrevocable thing and had killed a sentient being. Jen was a monster, but so was I. Weren't all supernaturals monsters to the mundanes?

That was all the time I allowed myself to contemplate Jen's demise. I would pay her some respects later. Now, I had a monster to kill.

I crawled to Harpe. Every muscle burned. Each breath like inhaling shards of glass. The blade, once soaked with Medusa's blood, was forever cursed to turn living things to stone.

Agony swept through me as I gripped the hilt of the blade and pushed to my feet. I probably had at least one fractured rib and a sprained if not broken ankle. With all the courage I could muster, I sprinted toward the tentacle, Harpe raised high.

I might die, but this monster wasn't going to destroy this beautiful city.

All my anger and fear exploded from my lungs in a shriek. My back spasmed. Fire blazed down the length of my spine. Thunder clapped. A zephyr lifted me. Suddenly, I was airborne and staying that way. In my periphery, golden wings flapped. I craned my neck around to see which harpy had rescued me. All I could see were the massive wings. It took another moment for my brain to catch up to what my body was doing. I had sprouted wings! I was flying.

I lifted my sword, unsteady in flight as a toddler walking. Less like a human toddler and more like a calf, who could walk instinctually once it had the hang of it.

I could fly!

Below Poseidon and Brad battled on, both looked weary. Ichor stained the floor. So many vessels lie about like dildo detritus. Seamen worked to put out fires or fight the tentacles. There was a key person missing. Amphitrite was supposed to be here defending her palace and city. Did she actually bail on her own domain?

I couldn't worry about that now.

I shrieked my fury over Jen's accidental death, over the gods tossing me about like I was a vessel not a person, and that my son, the next in line for oracle, would come to the same fate if I died here. I would make it out for Luke.

With all my might, I plunged harpe at an oncoming tentacle. Shock of impact reverberated up my arm.

The effort and pain were to no avail. The blade didn't pierce the hide of the tentacle. The tentacle however lashed back like a whip about to snap.

Hastily, I retreated—a really cool way of saying I flapped awkwardly to figure out how to fly backwards and up at the same time while trying to avoid the colossal tentacle.

The hide brushed against my feet, but I managed to up, up, up and away my way out of any injury.

The reprieve didn't last. An eye the size of a small building centered on a puce head that kinda reminded me of Patrick from that show Luke watched when he was a kid peered inside through the broken palace wall. A nightmarish beak several feet down from the giant eye cawed like a bird. The caw was loud enough and carried enough force to ruffle my feathers. Literally.

New to flying, I didn't know how to counter the air current. My body spun in dizzying directions as I struggled with control of my wings. Talk about learning on the job!

Finally, I managed to right myself and fly up and out of the palace, high, high, above. High enough I was out of reach from the beak blasts and the tentacles of the monster.

The thing had two of those giant eyes. It's massive features and torso were almost humanoid. Was it Scylla? If it was that legendary monster, we were in trouble. She was the sea monster who inspired the phrase "between Scylla and Charybdis", which would translate to English the colloquialism "between a rock and hard place."

The tentacles that weren't smashing the palace were tearing apart buildings. Seamen vessels got knocked out of the air as soon as they attempted to get close enough to laser beam the monster.

Think, Lydia. The creature had to have some sort of weakness.

Instead of answers, more questions occurred. Why was the creature attacking Atlantis? Why were Jen and Brad here?

It must have something to do with the Titans, the gate to Tartarus, and Poseidon pulling me through the gate to here. The gate must be some sort of door between universes. If oracles could read the skein made by the Fates. Maybe the skein was the fabric of reality itself, and oracles were tapping into some sort of path between worlds?

Dione, the first oracle, would know the answer. So would the Fates. I shuddered at the thought of meeting their personifications. Especially when they measured and cut the thread of people's lives.

I didn't want to harm the creature if I didn't have to. It seemed just a raging monster with no reason to kill but to kill, but I would be enraged too if someone imprisoned me in Tartarus. If only I had Phyr's mind control and planeswalking capabilities! I could calm the creature and send it to an ocean world or wherever it wouldn't do anyone harm.

However, I didn't have that luxury. Jen died because of the creature's blind rage. Seamen, who were only defending their home, were dead and dying. I *had* to kill the monster or more people would die for the sins of Zeus and the twelve against this Titan.

The flesh may not be penetrable, but the eye would be. I shook out my arms, readying myself. I couldn't do it alone. The eye would literally see me. The seamen were powerless against Scylla, and Poseidon was occupied by Brad. Amphitrite was nowhere to be seen.

I didn't want to endanger Nicky or the other harpies, but they could provide a distraction. I wasn't skilled enough at fighting to attack the monster without help.

I cried out. I didn't know if it would work, but I screamed for harpies to come join me.

I waited, hovering in place. I was sore and tired, but I couldn't give up. The only other choice was to go back down and go it alone.

My gaze swept across the city to the waterfall in the far distance. I could also possibly find the crack between worlds Poseidon opened for me.

I shook my head. No. I would help Atlantis. Besides, who knew where Typhon would take Scylla next? The last thing Earth needed was a pissed off sea monster. We had our own problems.

Something near the waterfall caught my eye. A figure as large as Typhon, no larger, *much* larger emerged.

Harpe in hand, I braced myself to face a legend.

CHAPTER

ELEVEN

The massive entity split apart into many creatures. At the familiar sound of the harpies' battle cry, I released my breath in a loud whoosh. Help was on its way.

I flew to meet the harpies.

Nicky met me halfway, followed by all the harpies from Milagro Bay and more I didn't recognize. Lukie wasn't with them. He didn't have wings yet. First, my stepmother looked at me and my big ol' wings with an air of such pride. Second, her gaze swept to the battle raging far below.

"Scylla is free from Tartarus," she said, shock limning her voice.

"Yes. I need you to distract her while I go for her eye."

Unexpectedly, Nicky didn't command the harpies to do anything. Instead, she paled and asked, "Where is Charybdis?"

I shrugged. Well, I did the best shrugging I could while hovering. I was still getting the hang of flight.

"I haven't seen any massive tidal waves or whirlpools. Just beaks and tentacles."

"That must be Amphitrite's doing. The goddess of the sea has grown in power since Charybdis's imprisonment."

Ah, so that was why I didn't see Amphitrite. I'd assumed the queen took a hike. Goes to show just because someone isn't your cup of tea doesn't mean they're all bad.

"Poseidon as well. He should be able to stop Scylla easily. Where is he?"

I gestured to the palace. "Battling Typhon down there."

"If he's any match for Poseidon, Typhon has been free for longer than we suspected."

Scylla roared below. Massive tentacles crashing against buildings Godzilla style.

"I have Harpe," I declared once the noise died down to distant battle sounds. "It was once soaked in Medusa's blood and turned Echidna to stone. If you all provide a distraction, I'll go for Scylla's eye."

Nicky eyed the sword. A strange look passing over her face. There and gone. She shouted orders to her flock. Then shouted to the newcomers. A plan was in place. Now, all I had to do was turn Scylla to stone without getting killed.

Harpies divided into units. Each unit targeted a tentacle. Their paralyzing shrieks filled the air. Unlike Scylla's sonic blasts, harpy screeches didn't affect me. However, the sea monster shuddered. She cawed and roared in return.

Soon, dolphin and eel vessels joined the harpies in their organized attack.

I watched and waited, selecting the right moment to join. When Scylla seemed impossibly overwhelmed, I dove. A small, unnoticed figure among the chaos, I kept my focus sharp and harpe pointed at my target. I circled left and right, avoiding the sea monster's gaze. When I struck her eye, I drove harpe in with such force that my entire arm sunk in the flesh. The texture was a mixture of viscous fluid and gelatin.

Ew! Disgust replaced fear and rage, but not for long.

The sea monster didn't go down easily. She cawed and roared batting away the forces surrounding her tentacles.

Oh crap. I want off this ride.

I pulled and pulled trying to free myself. I swung with her petrifying eye as I tried to pull my arm and harpe out. My arm seemed only to sink deeper. To make matters worse, the living material surrounding harpe quickly hardened, solidifying into stone.

Shit. Shit. Shit!

Panic overrode the adrenaline of hitting my mark. If I didn't free my arm, I'd lose it. If I were stuck in the petrified remains of Scylla, would I too turn to stone?

Nicky flew to my side. "Let go of your sword!"

"No! It's an heirloom."

It would be easier to let go, but I couldn't lose the sword. I'd been entrusted with it by my grandparents. Yiayia and Papus kept good care of these things because they'd been in my family for centuries upon centuries.

"Stubborn child!"

I'd argue that I was over forty years old, but she was ancient. "Name calling won't help."

She gripped my arm. Together we yanked.

I felt a little give and the scrape of metal against stone. "It's working."

"Call them to you. Some aren't mine."

Understanding who she meant, I shrieked for the harpies to come to my aid. As she predicted, the harpies arrived. Each grabbing me here and there. Some grabbing the harpy holding me creating a chain of harpies. With a sickening sucking sound and a wet *POP*, my arm came free, harpe still in my grasp.

Even without the blade within her, Scylla rapidly petrified. First her eye hardened, then her head, and then the tentacles stilled until there was nothing but a statue of what had been a mighty sea monster.

The harpies whooped and cheered. The seamen honked their phallic-shaped vessels.

I should feel victorious too, but an ache curled in my chest, squeezing. Tears, hot and wet, dampened my cheeks.

Nicky squeezed my free hand. "You won your first battle. Yet, you don't look like a victor."

"The lives of two great legends ended after how many thousands of years of existence? Why? Because Zeus and his brothers want to reign over three worlds and be worshipped by humans? That doesn't feel like victory."

Nicky flew closer, pushing a stray hair from my face. "A harpy's wings sprout when she decides to be a protector. Were you protecting Zeus and his brothers?"

"Maybe Poseidon a little," I admit, but didn't say that I felt a kinship to him.

Some unreadable emotion flickered on Nicky's face, replaced again by empathy. "I doubt it was just for him."

"I mostly fought so the innocents who live here wouldn't be harmed. Scylla was all rage and beyond reason. I was also afraid that she might break through to my world. We're not ready for a sea Titan. She would put innocents in danger and make all supes look like monsters."

She smiled. "There. That is your reason to go on and not let what happened today consume you. There will be more battles as Titans slip from Tartarus."

I exhaled a long shuddering breath and nodded. Nicky was right. I didn't like killing or battle, but I also didn't like innocents being harmed. The Olympians chose me to be their Oracle, but I chose to be a harpy for those who couldn't fight for themselves.

CHAPTER

TWELVE

By the time I returned to the palace to see how Poseidon and Typhon's battle turned out, the Titan and the remains of his wife Echidna had disappeared. Poseidon didn't provide much of an explanation as to what happened other than Typhon yielded and took his bride.

"He wasn't here for the same reasons as Scylla," was all the King of Atlantis would offer.

Two seamen approached. One carried a sack of gold and jewels, handing it to their king.

He, in turn, handed the sack to me. "For your part in the battle and to pay your harpies."

I almost declined, but then I came to my senses. Olympus paid me a monthly stipend, but the harpies risked their lives and should be compensated.

Amphitrite returned, too. The queen looked much more haggard than she appeared when we spoke earlier.

"Charybdis relented," the queen announced.

Poseidon rushed to his wife's side, forgetting me.

While they had their moment. I gave the harpies who came to

67

my aid leave to return home and paid them, dividing the contents of the sack. Some lingered, unsure of leaving me here in Atlantis, i.e., not my territory without an escort. Nicky assured them she'd take me home and ordered her harpies to leave.

Her face grew solemn, and her eyes glistened as if she wanted to cry. "We must return you to Hades. Persephone will fret about you after you disappeared, as will Lucinda."

Exhausted to the marrow, aching everywhere, and still healing from open wounds in a few places, going back to the gates of Tartarus wasn't something I wanted to do.

As if reading my mind, Nicky added, "You know how much I don't want to go there. However, Lucinda said that her queen has taken a liking to you. Persephone doesn't do that often. It's best not to upset her."

"Far be it from me to upset the gods," I muttered, feeling as cranky as a child who'd skipped naptime. Part of me knew I had to go to Olympus too. This wasn't Zeus's domain, but he liked to know things.

A streak of fire zipping across the sky caught my attention. Everyone cleaning up stopped what they were doing to watch as it hurtled toward the palace.

Sliding Harpe from its sheathe, I braced for another attack.

A man—or rather a man-shaped being since human men couldn't fly around on fire—landed on the stone remnant of Scylla, and then hopped down to the palace floor.

The flames doused until only a very pissed off Hermes in full, golden armor, wings spread, and a sword covered in gore remained.

My heart fluttered a bit at the site of the god. He was always so subdued in my old Victorian, dressing in sweats and t-shirts or track-suits like a regular person. Right now, Hermes was in full Olympian mode. I had to admit. The badass warrior god look did things for me. I'd blame my grandparents for filling my head with stories about the gods, but no other god stirred something I'd thought long dead inside me. It was Hermes with that "I'll kill you all if you hurt her" expression.

He took in the scene until his dark gaze landed on me. Whatever he saw, propelled him to me faster than my eyes could track.

His hands cradled my face. I hadn't even seen when or where he put away his shield and sword. "Are you injured?"

"Pretty banged up." I grinned and glanced at the petrified Scylla. "But, not as bad as the other guy."

Hermes smiled back. His adoration lighting up the entire room. The smile dropped as a downpour of people-sized infernos dropped from the sky, morphing into Olympians.

Zeus in gold and silver armor, helmet, and shield spattered with inky ichor held a glowing lightning bolt. Hera, dressed much the same, joined her husband. Ares grinned as if he were happy to be covered in gore. Apollo was less of a mess but looking surlier than I remembered. Artemis had her bow ready. Athena had a sword and Aegis, she too looked as if she'd sliced up a few Titans.

All of them seemed angrier than a cat dunked in a pool. They'd come from a fight and were ready to pick another.

Zeus stomped toward Poseidon. "There was an attack on Olympus, or we would have answered your distress call sooner."

So, Poseidon had called for help. Interesting.

Somehow the bags of gold seemed like a pittance now. The harpies and I had saved Atlantis. I let it roll off my back. We hadn't done it for pay.

Hera took me in, and then her gaze swung to Hermes, noting our proximity.

I, in turn, noticed how close Apollo had landed to her, almost shielding her even now. Since when did Hera like any of Zeus's extramarital progeny? I didn't have time to question it further.

Pillars of black smoke burst from the floor. The smoke cleared, revealing sirens covered in blood and gore, Persephone and her husband arrived in battle gear. Cerberus loped at their heels, all three heads, snarling and vicious.

I took a sharp breath. Not because of the hound I considered my dog.

I'd expected the king of the Underworld to appear grim and old, not ... *wowzah*. With, thick and shiny jet-black hair, chiseled jawline, a full, sensuous mouth, and dark eyes with sweeping lashes, Aidoneus, commonly referred to by his title of Hades, was the handsomest of the three brothers. No wonder vain Zeus sent his brother to reign in the Underworld. The king of the gods likely wanted the hottie competition as far away as possible.

The king and queen of the Underworld well matched. Persephone, a fierce and vibrant force of nature, next to her dark and mysterious husband.

They didn't look like lovebirds at the moment. They appeared as warrior rulers, ready to battle for their ally. The queen's gaze landed on me. A quick sweep over my person before her dark eyes turned to her uncle, Poseidon, and then, the petrified Scylla. Lastly, the goddess narrowed her gaze on Zeus.

If Persephone had any affection for her father, her expression didn't display it now. Anger sharpened the angles of her lovely face. She spoke in a clear, authoritative tone of a queen, accusation limning her every word. "There was a breach in the gate of Tartarus. We had to deploy the harpy and siren armies to guard it," Persephone declared, her gaze swinging again to me and my *harpy* wings. "I'd believed Dione 's plot had been thwarted. Why haven't you managed your affairs, *Father*?"

I drew in a different sort of sharp breath.

Hermes positioned himself closer to me, hand gripping me. "If they fight, I'm getting you out of here," he whispered. "Please don't debate me on it."

I wouldn't. Let the gods tear each other up, as long as they didn't harm innocents.

Zeus inhaled and straightened his shoulders. He bore her accusation with a look of wrathful indignation fitting the king of the gods.

"How dare you accuse me when it is you and your husband's domain that has been breached?"

Aidoneus's face darkened. Actually, his entire presence evoked, *"I'm big scary Hades, not your brother Aidoneus right now. Fuck around and find out, Zeus."*

The king of the gods sneered. "Is this some sort of poorly attempted coup, brother? You hide behind your wife, silent and threatening, but almost reticent. Let us believe you're the victims too. All the while the whole attack on Atlantis and Olympus is some sort of machination on your part. You created chaos so that you can claim me incompetent and take my throne."

Maybe Zeus was on to something. Persephone didn't want anyone to know she was helping me. She also encouraged me to use the gate as a way to manifest my powers.

"Why would I want to rule Olympus? My queen and I are more widely celebrated by mortals now. Temples are being erected in our honor all over." He gestured to me. "We don't need recruiters." He then enlisted Poseidon, "If he weakens our domains, his position strengthens."

The three brothers flung a flurry of wild accusations at each other. It felt like being at a function for my ex's family. They always talked on top of each other as they argued. Everyone wanted to make their point, and none of them were listening, therefore, not communicating.

I stepped around Hermes. One thing I've learned from fighting the Titans is that when I screamed, it got their undivided attention. So, I let loose a shriek that would make any harpy proud.

The gods covered their ears or winced, but the screech did its job. All eyes turned to me.

"Have you ever heard the term divide and conquer?" I met the gaze of the three kings and queens. "Someone is letting the Titans out, or maybe, just maybe mortal belief has strengthened them enough to break free. Either way, if you fight among yourselves over this, you lose your greatest strength, the united front you posed against the old gods. You should rebuild and plan your defenses, not squabble."

Athena stepped forward. Her light brown, almost blonde hair twisted high from her stoic face. Arachne's former crush and now enemy possessed an austere countenance. Golden brown eyes filled with penetrating intelligence homed their gaze on me.

Glacial frissons with a razor-sharp bite skittered down my spine. Every god listened to Athena's judgement. The last time she judged me, she called me, or rather all Oracles, liars. Judging by the derision in her sneer, I doubted she'd have anything complimentary to say now.

As if she addressed a legion of soldiers on the battlefield, her voice carried loud and clear when she declared, "The Oracle is right."

I opened my mouth to protest and promptly clamped it shut. *Did she say what I thought she'd said?* I'd love the fae ability to communicate telepathically right now so I could ask Hermes.

The shock on the Olympian, Atlantean, and Underworld faces confirmed the goddess of freaking wisdom had supported me.

I wondered why.

Athena answered my question in her next breath. "Which means we have a traitor in our midst. Someone standing here is responsible for the breach in the gates of Tartarus. They wish to cause discord among us. We can eliminate the three kingly brothers. Each of them lost greatly from this attack, and their rulership has been drawn into question."

"Perhaps this was Dione's plan all along," Apollo suggested, fervor in his tone. He swept his arm in a gesture that illuminated all those present.

Neat trick.

The sun god's tone grew more impassioned as he continued, "She wanted to sow the seeds of discord among us so that we're all in a state of distrust when the real attack begins. Have we all forgotten she was not one of us, but a Titan? Dione stands to benefit the most. Her brethren, her own children are among those imprisoned. She must have been planning this since their imprisonment."

Athena didn't respond, she only set her calculating gaze upon her half brother.

"One thing hasn't made sense to me," I said, while the siblings stared each other down. "Dione warned me that danger was coming before Echidna kidnapped me, but then she showed up with them. Why bother warning me if she was in on it?" I watched Hera's face for a reaction. Dione suspected the queen of the gods to be in on some conspiracy, but I wasn't going to point fingers without solid evidence.

"Not quite," Hermes replied. "Dione was waiting for us when we arrived, which was customary for training the new Oracle, but Echidna and Typhon showed up shortly after."

I'd assumed they'd been hiding, but Typhon wasn't small enough to duck behind a building while we drove into town. They likely took some hidden door like Hermes.

"Father, since a key part in this machination involves the Oracle, I would like to request to accompany Lydia to Earth. Along with Hermes, of course."

"I, too, wish to protect the Oracle," Persephone said. "I would like to gift her Cerberus and the use of my siren general, who is our agent there in the archangel's council and keeps an eye on the mundane authorities."

Though her expression gave nothing away, Lucinda paled. Her gaze flicked to me, but only briefly.

I bet the siren didn't want me knowing that nugget of truth. These gods might be at each other's throats, but at the end of the day, they were all from the same ilk. "Of the ichor" is what Hermes's sister, the water nymph, had called me because somewhere along the line, I was the Olympians' family, too. Their track record with kin wasn't appealing.

"Admiral Cosmo," Poseidon bellowed.

A melusina, or rather a seaman soldier from Poseidon's Mighty

Eel Navy broke from their ranks, sliding upon his fishtails to report to his king. Linebacker shoulders and massive arms topped a seaman almost as big as the King of Atlantis himself. The seaman uniform clung to a muscular torso like latex. His silver hair was braided into a faux-hawk style fin on top of his head, adorned with gold and silver rings. More rings decorated his beard forked into two plates.

Cosmo bowed before his king. "Your Majesty?"

"You will guard the Oracle with your life," Poseidon declared, his gaze sweeping from the petrified form of Scylla to me. "I owe Lydia that much."

Cosmo regarded me, projecting deep respect from every fiber of his big body. He then bowed to his king. "For you, my king, and because she saved all that I hold dear, I swear upon my life to protect Lydia Kourakos from all harm."

My eyes stung. I couldn't help but be moved by his oath. Out of the cadre of gods and supernaturals coming to protect me, only Hermes and this seaman wanted to protect *me*, Lydia, not "the Oracle."

CHAPTER
THIRTEEN

Being the god of the crossroads, Hermes led the whole party from Atlantis to the driveway behind my house. I was grateful he didn't take us directly into the house. Given we had Athena, Hermes, Cerberus, Lucinda, Cosmo, and myself, the group was too big to just walk into any room. At least Poseidon granted Cosmo human legs for when he walked on land to fit in. Hopefully, we didn't have a *Splash!* situation and getting the seaman wet would make him half fish again. Because we had a large number of people, I needed to confer with Arachne where we would put everyone. A former priestess, she was better at these things than I was.

Crap.

Arachne didn't know Athena was coming.

The door to the back of the house swung open, smacking the wall. Someone burst through the threshold in a joyful sprint. Her long dreads bounced, and her copper-colored eyes shone with the adoration of the devout.

Double crap.

In the chaos, I'd forgotten about Nora, Athena's devotee and our houseguest. She practically tripped over her own feet as she bounded down the back porch steps.

Following her, Luke casually strolled out. Arachne exited with an abundance of caution.

While Nora greeted the goddess by throwing herself on the ground and prostrating herself, my other housemate and Athena's former friend took her time shutting the door behind her with a gentle click.

Athena seemed to not even notice Nora. Her dark gaze on Arachne. The goddess's expression was stoic at her warmest, but right now her face could freeze boiling water instantly.

"Arachne is my assistant at the temple," I explained.

Hermes put himself between his sister and her former friend, careful to avoid stepping on the now sobbing and still prostrate Nora. "I brought Arachne here to protect the Oracle and teach Lydia, who had no formal temple training."

Athena's gaze focused past Hermes on Arachne as she said, "She's an excellent priestess. Lydia will receive the best-quality instruction. As long as no one goes missing, I can see no harm in it."

My housemate's lip quivered. The praise coupled with the insult must be awful to bare.

The goddess's eyes dropped to Nora. "I assume you've brought us to a dwelling for priestesses who do not inhabit the temple itself."

"Besides Arachne, myself, and Nora here. You're looking at the priestesses. Harpies act as ushers and bodyguards. They all live in their own homes, though."

Athena cracked a hint of a smile, her eyes again on Arachne. My housemate remained at her position by the door.

"I expect there will be much that has changed since I last tread the mortal world. Therefore, I come here not only as your protector, but as a pupil to learn. The past is in the past."

Arachne nodded once. "I'll get all of your rooms ready."

Athena inclined her head, in gracious acknowledgement.

Then the goddess of wisdom, crouched next to the sobbing Nora.

She ran her long fingers over her worshipper's head. "Nike Nora Jones, I have heard your prayers. I am here. Things will change for the better. Rise. We have much to do."

Nora did as she was bidden, the adoration and awe in her pretty face hard to watch.

As we all made our way to the house, led by Nora holding hands with Athena, I worried my lip. I hoped Athena wasn't the traitor and had pulled a fast one by coming here. If she were, she'd put herself in a fantastic position.

With the goddess occupied, Luke approached. His eyes were wide with shock as we embraced. "Ma, you have wings."

"I do. I have no idea how to put them away." I suddenly wanted them to no longer be there. Blades of fire seared down my back. A thousand ants crawled under my flesh. Within moments, the pain was gone, and so were my wings.

WHILE ARACHNE AND Nora busied themselves opening up rooms for Lucinda, Athena, and Cosmo, Luke showed our extended guests to the dining room. Juan had cooked for an army last night and we had plenty of arroz con pollo to sate us. Fighting had made everyone hungry.

I sat at the head of a table with a god at either side, a siren in her human form, and a seaman gifted with human legs. Life certainly was strange sometimes.

Except for the occasional murmur of appreciation, we ate in silence. Cosmo seemed the least acquainted with silverware. The seaman used Arachne's homemade pita bread Luke had brought out to scoop up the rice dish. Intent on their own meal and exhausted from battle, no one cared.

I occasionally felt Cosmo's eyes on me, but he seemed more interested in his surroundings than anyone at the table.

Lucinda furiously texted on her phone. So bizarre to see her on the modern device wearing the ancient-looking siren armor in my dining room. At least she was back in human form.

Hermes grinned when I looked in his direction. His eyes warm while something else lingered there. Longing.

Guess the battle look on me did things for him as well.

I would never get over the god's romantic admiration for me. My heart fluttered like I was a teenager, not old enough to have a grown son. My body lit up in a way it never had before, even with the post battle exhaustion, or because of the battle. Suddenly, I wanted to do things.

I could've died today, but I didn't. I was alive and glad of it. I ate with gusto and flirted, winking at Hermes when no one was looking.

By the time we finished with our meal, Arachne and Nora appeared, ready to show everyone to their rooms. I excused myself to my own bedroom so I could take a shower and change out of my bloody and tattered clothes. I didn't go alone. Hermes followed.

"Can I come in?" he asked.

Oh, he could. He could come in. I was weary, but there was something about surviving the fight that made me want to celebrate being alive.

"I need to shower."

Why did I say that? Oh, right. I was covered in blood, ichor, and nasty dried-up eyeball gunk. However, I wasn't sure if he wanted to talk or get into bed. We hadn't done the deed yet because I wasn't ready to commit after a long, unhappy marriage.

He posted a hand on the doorframe and grinned. His other hand settled on my hip and squeezed. "As do I."

My jaw dropped. I stammered for a minute, my brain needing to catch up with the implications. "Uh, you said you don't want to have sex until, I'm sure."

"We're adults. I'm sure we can control ourselves."

"We'll see about that." It was my turn to grin as I opened the door and backed inside.

CHAPTER

FOURTEEN

The lock clicked after Hermes shut the door behind him. He breached the distance between us faster than a blink. Hands found my hips. His mouth crushed mine in a bruising kiss.

I gave as equally as I got, emboldened by this display of passion.

He broke off long enough to say, "You are magnificent, slaying a Titan with so little training."

Wonder limned every word.

My stomach clenched. "I didn't want to. She made me kill Jen and would have destroyed the city. Innocents would have died."

His dark eyes grew serious. "That is the magnificent part. A true warrior doesn't fight for conquest or glory. She fights to protect those who cannot fend for themselves, and she never enjoys taking a life. My sister was never meant to be a war goddess, but the ancient Greek generals chose Athena's wisdom to help them defend their home."

I always thought it was awesome that Athena had her own city, her own statue and a depiction of her birth were the featured items of the Parthenon. A goddess born a grown woman, dressed in full armor, ready to defend herself and those who sought her protection. It made me recall that even after Athena had once fought her uncle Poseidon for control of Athens and *won*, she shared the city with him.

The recollection gave me hope that the goddess wasn't the one trying to usurp the three brothers by releasing the Titans. Athena loved her family, and judging by the way they all listened to her, they loved and respected her.

In thanks for the reminder and in genuine happiness that he held me in as high of regard as Athena, I kissed Hermes as hard as he'd kissed me. My clothes dropped to the floor, released by speedy fingers.

His clothes followed at a slower pace.

I took a step back, letting him see all of me. My heart raced, and my skin blazed as he drank me in. My body didn't have the muscled perfection of an Olympian, but the way Hermes's eyes darkened with desire and the swipe of his tongue across his shapely lips made me feel perfect.

"You are marvelous to behold," he said in Greek.

"You're not too shabby yourself."

That was the understatement of the century. Hermes was, in a word, magnificent. His dark olive skin covered a lean but well-muscled body. Springy black hair covered his legs and a narrow trail of the same hair led from his navel to his Olympic-sized *joy*. The messenger of the gods was very, very happy to see me naked and ready to deliver his package.

"I can control myself," Hermes said, breaking me from my ogling trance as he led me to my private bathroom. "Let's get cleaned up."

I didn't think I'd be able to promise the same, and I was right not to do so. Things got a lot steamier once we hit the shower.

A HAND GRIPPED my butt and squeezed as I turned on the shower. I let the water heat up and turned around.

I crossed my arms over my chest and clucked my tongue. "I thought you could control yourself."

He grinned, brown eyes lighting up with mischief. "I am. If I weren't, that would've been my mouth."

Need coiled tight within me. I unfolded my arms and touched his hard chest. So much delicious muscle covering every inch of him. I let my hand wander over the planes, hills, and valleys.

Hermes reached past me, testing the water. "It's warm."

"And wet," I replied.

He lifted me over the rim of the clawed foot tub and placed me in the shower as if I weighed nothing. Then the god joined me, long legs swinging over the rim as if it were a small obstacle, not a few feet deep.

The water soaked my hair and body, but I hardly noticed the spray. All my attention centered on the god before me. We were really going to do this.

"Can I wash you?"

I laughed. Not because I thought the offer was funny. Despite the enormous evidence of his desire and my own need growing to the same level, I was nervous. I hadn't slept with anyone but Carlo. It didn't help that Hermes was one of my girlhood crushes, and here he was asking to wash me.

"I haven't had anyone wash me since I was a baby," I admitted.

It was his turn to cluck his tongue. "Time to remedy that."

Hermes started with my hair, tenderly taking his time to lather my drenched curls. He massaged my scalp and combed his fingers through the tangles the right way, as if he'd tended my hair his whole life—or at least had spent a lot of time thinking about how he'd do it given the chance.

The thought that he fantasized about doing this undid me in ways I never dreamed I'd feel.

I've had nice and relaxing shampoo and conditioning treatments at salons, but I wasn't attracted to my hair stylists, and it wasn't sensual. Also, they weren't naked and pressing their body against me. Would've had some lawsuits if they did. However, between me and Hermes, it was completely appropriate and totally hot.

The god took his time washing my face and neck. I stood under the shower, closing my eyes to rinse. Even under the spray, I could hear his sharp inhale.

I let him get under the warm spray, and he pulled me to him, kissing me. I slid my tongue between his lip. We made love with our mouths until we were both breathless.

Hermes drew back, expression as love drunk as I felt. His voice was deeper, gravelly with need as he said, "I'm not done. You're still dirty."

Casting my gaze downward, I agreed. "Oh, you have no idea."

Again, he took his time, massaging body wash over every part. Water cascaded off his gleaming muscles and soaked his curls, stretching the hair into long locks framing his chiseled face. The reverence in his handsome features combined with his firm but gentle caresses made me lose all sense of modesty, embarrassment. I'd never felt so wanton and so desirable in my life.

We switched places, allowing for me to be under the water to rinse off and get myself under control. I wanted to respect his wish to not go all the way until I was ready to give him some sort of commitment, but it was so, so hard.

Pun intended.

If the way he washed me was any clue to what kind of lover Hermes would be, I was in for a treat. I could still have a little fun for the both of us.

"Your turn," I said, smiling wide. Which wasn't the smartest thing to do in the shower. Water trickled in between my teeth.

Nostrils flaring, Hermes nodded his consent.

Not expecting company, I only had my products. "I don't have a manly scent."

Hermes leaned over, kissed my cheek and spoke softly against my ear, "I know."

I laughed. "I mean my soap smells flowery and sweet."

He smoothed his palms over my waist and gripped my hips. "I like flowery and sweet. I plan on having your scent all over me by the time we're done anyway."

His lips found mine.

The water was a bit too much for me, so I reached behind me and switched off the water from the shower head to tub faucet. With a toe, I pushed down the stopper.

"Sit," I commanded.

Being much shorter than the god, Hermes had to sit in the tub so that I could wash his hair. Most of the gross stuff had already rinsed off. Must be nice to only need water to be clean.

He chuckled and did as I commanded. I grabbed what I needed from the shower caddy and placed them within reach in the corner.

With very little coaxing from Hermes, I sat, straddling his legs. His length pressed against my belly as he leaned forward to kiss me on the mouth.

I made him turn around and sat behind him, lathering his hair and raking my fingers through the dense curls much the same way he did mine.

I massaged his neck and shoulders next. His moan in response sent shivers of anticipatory delight straight to my core. This was as much a treat for me as it was for him. I lathered his back, taking my sweet time as he did. After rinsing there, I reached around to work his chest and arms. Then I moved to the ridges of his abdomen.

Except for a cursory sweep of a soapy hand between my legs, he hadn't touched me in my most intimate spot.

"Can I wash your cock?"

Hermes's exhale came out in a loud whoosh. His voice a low growl, when he replied, "Lydia, all I am is yours. Wash whatever you like."

I poured more soap on one hand while the other gripped him.

As my hand slid down his length, Hermes let out a guttural sound that made me clench deep within. It was the sexiest noise I'd ever heard, and I couldn't wait to make him make it again.

Hermes let me play. By the sound he made "let" was not the correct word.

Through gritted teeth, he said, "enough."

Disappointed he didn't orgasm, but respecting his wishes, I disentangled myself and stood, ready to get out and get dressed. Playtime over.

"Don't go."

When I turned around, his eyes burned into me with desire, and I was aflame.

"I want to kiss you," he said in a husky voice, sliding a hand up my inner thigh. Reaching the apex, he added. "Here. Don't worry. I won't let you fall."

I nodded, so excited I couldn't speak.

Hermes kissed my hip just above my thigh, working his way until he was where I ached for him. With each swipe of his tongue, he sent ripples of pleasure through me, winding me tighter and tighter until I unraveled for him.

My legs were like jelly, as I rode echoes of the initial orgasm. Hermes gripped me tight so I wouldn't fall.

"I need you now." His voice was low and gravelly, eyes filled with that need.

"Have me."

With lightning speed, he rose and lifted me off my feet. We were out of the tub and onto my bed so fast, my head spun.

He spread my legs apart, pausing to meet my hungry gaze. "Do you want this, Lydia?"

"Yes." I was so ready to do this, I almost begged him.

He lowered himself over me, aligning himself at my entrance. "I'm a fool to ask you for forever when I could lose you or die myself in the battles ahead. I know you do not love me as I love you, but I will do everything I can to win your heart so thoroughly you'll never want another."

Looking me in the eyes, Hermes thrust inside me. Filling every inch. He stayed like that for a moment, allowing me to adjust to his girth. Then he set a languid pace. I wrapped my legs around his hips, pulling him back in each time he withdrew.

I wound and wound tighter until I wrung out, climaxing again.

Hermes picked up the pace, before stilling completely and crying out my name. The god crumpled atop me, spent. Then rolled off and pulled me to him, cradling me against his body.

Sated and happy, my eyelids grew heavy. "That was incredible."

Hermes kissed the back of my head. "There's so much more I'd like to show you. For now, you should get some sleep, my love."

As if his words were a spell, I did.

CHAPTER

FIFTEEN

When I was young and moving from town to town along the eastern seaboard because Carlo had made some enemy or had botched some scheme, I knew I'd never have the sort of life my grandparents lived. I had my quiet time while he was off running with his crew, but there was never a golden years' image of Carlo and me. I didn't like to think of the future because the future seemed to be more unpaid bills, not a sense of establishment or security.

Now, I had my own home and enough money to pay the bills and then some, I found myself brushing my teeth next to a naked god. Okay. Hermes was wearing a towel draped around his hips, but there was very little left to the imagination under the pink, seashell-patterned terrycloth.

If I kept this job as Oracle, I would live forever as forty-something. Arachne was an old woman and immortal. Nicky stayed looking like she was in her thirties. Zeus and Poseidon, grayed and a little wizened, appeared as if they were in their midfifties. Dione had been an elegant woman in her sixties. With immortality came no quiet years.

Did I really want to be an Oracle forever? Did I have a future with Hermes? What would that look like?

Hermes wrapped his arms around me and kissed me on the neck just behind the ear, breaking me from my pensive mood. "Does your mind ever quiet?"

I spat out my toothpaste and rinsed with a cup of water before spitting that out too. After wiping my mouth, I turned within his embrace to face him. "Always thinking ten steps ahead, kept me alive, and a roof over my head."

He smiled, but it didn't reach his eyes. He'd watched me struggle and was told to not intervene. "Am I privy to this morning's machinations?"

"Has anyone retired from the position of Oracle, and grown old and died naturally?"

Hermes grinned. "Usually, I get that question after they've been Oracle for at least twenty years or more."

I snickered. "Well, I'm asking now and would like an answer—" I looked at my watch. "Oh, about now."

The god brushed my hair aside. "Only if she is incompetent of mind, and you are not incompetent of *anything*, my treasure."

My treasure.

Now that was an endearment I could get used to. "Why didn't anyone tell me that was an option before?"

Sadness limned his chiseled features, making him tragically beautiful. "Because you'd have to be out of control of your faculties. That is not a state I'd like to think about, and if you were ill in that way, the mantle would be passed, and you'd grow old and die. I want you around for as long as I am." He kissed my forehead. "All of the wonderful mind, inside this pretty head, intact."

"Yeah, but why didn't Dione tell me the Oracle mantle could be passed on to someone else while I was alive?"

Hermes grimaced. He didn't want to continue down this road, but I did. I couldn't control the gift and "see" what I told others. Every story my grandparents told me had a moral of the gods being fickle with their favor. My lack of control could mean death since I would hold no value to the gods as someone with the power to open the gates to Tartarus.

"Because we'd thought there was no one else." Hermes sighed. "The ichor is too weak in all the other lines descended from Dione, except for you and your mother. There's no one."

A new fear arose. "What about Lukie?"

Hermes lowered his voice. "Luke wasn't accounted for. There's never been an Oracle that was a man, even if he was assigned female at birth."

Luke didn't want to be Oracle. He's said as much many times to anyone who would listen. He wanted the life he and Juan had made for themselves back, not to be forever entwined in his extended family's drama. I didn't blame him. If I'd had any kind of life, I wouldn't have signed my name in blood and took off across the country to dangers and treasures unknown.

I had to figure out this power and fast, or me and my son would both be in trouble.

Hermes hooked my chin with his finger, lifting my face, and thus my gaze, to meet his. His dark eyes brimmed with concern. "I do not want to be simply your lover. I want to be your confident and you mine. Tell me your worries and let us bear this burden together."

Okay, I'm starting to see why women went gaga for gods. Carlo would see worry on my face and start getting defensive, thinking I was about to accuse him of something. Generally, he had been the cause of most of my worry instead of my partner in this world in the truest sense. Tears stung the backs of my eyes.

So many people had entrusted me with their concerns, their hopes, their fears, but I never had that. My grandparents were elderly and infirm. Before they passed, I was their caretaker. I couldn't burden them. I never had a partner or friends. Even Luke was my kid. It was my job as his mom to be the rock. I had to be strong for him.

I blew out my breath and decided to trust Hermes, taking his word as truth and not pretty things to keep me. "I can't actually see the future."

"Yes, you can. I was there when you've made predictions."

"I tried to become a true Oracle like my mother and those who came before me. The last prophecy came out of my mouth, but I can't understand the language I speak when I make a prophecy. I'm not controlling it at all. It's like a piece of me is disconnected from the rest."

I expected him to back away and cut his ties. I'm a bad bet. Faulty. Not in control of my Oracle faculties. Instead, Hermes listened and didn't reply right away.

"There are two people who could help. One is Dione, who we cannot access for many reasons. Another is Hecate. She knows the most about magic. If you choose to not share this secret with the other gods, we'll have to slip out of your multiple guardians' watchful eyes to see the latter."

I grinned. "Like a secret mission? Do we get code names? I've always wanted to be a Bond girl. Well, actually, I wanted to be 007."

He'd watched some movies with me, so Hermes understood the reference. His shapely lips curved into a handsome smile, but his amusement didn't reach his eyes. "Yes. Like one of your screenplays and with all the dangers involved in a clandestine quest. Hecate is not," He pauses. "Always a pleasant person, especially since she announced she wanted to rest."

I worry my lip. The last thing I wanted to do is anger Hecate. She was an ancient Titan who chose to live in the Underworld. "Alright, as soon as we get a chance to slip away."

He smiled, his eyes crinkling to half-moons. He leaned in to kiss me. Before our lips met, he whispered, "So brave."

Or desperate.

I kept the thought to myself.

CHAPTER

SIXTEEN

ermes and I came down to the dining room together in the company of Cerberus, who had apparently slept across the threshold to my room all night. The hound was in his singular-head, black Labrador form, panting and drooling his way downstairs. Excited I was awake, he almost tripped me several times.

Heads bowed together, Athena and Nora sat at the dining table. They spoke in low tones.

I gave Hermes a look as we continued past the dining room.

He shrugged. If he wasn't worried about it, neither was I.

We found Luke and Juan in the kitchen, leaning against the counter and sipping coffee. The couple set their gazes on Cosmo, who sat at the table contemplating his bowl of oatmeal. His expression oozed suspicion.

Arachne and Lucinda were nowhere to be seen, which troubled me. Arachne was an early riser. A mother and a siren, Lucinda didn't seem to be the type to stay in bed late. "Where's your auntie?"

"Showing Lucinda the garden," Luke replied. His eyes still focused on Cosmo.

The seaman plunged his spoon in the bowl and then lifted it slowly, inspecting the dripping mush.

"It tastes better than it looks," Hermes offered. "Well, better than the gruel that the mortals used to eat."

Cosmo turned a dubious gaze to the god and then to me.

Even though I'd never had porridge from the past, I nodded encouragingly.

His expression changed. Expression solemn, he took a gulping bite, swallowing the oatmeal as if it were a sacred duty.

"If you don't like it. You can eat something else," I told Cosmo in Greek, trying not to laugh as I took two mugs out of the cupboard.

"No. This meal is sufficient, and I am grateful for it," Cosmo vowed in Greek.

Luke's face turned red as if he was holding his breath to keep from laughing.

Cosmo lifted the bowl and slurped the oatmeal, making sounds of enjoyment that were ... rather suggestive out of context.

Luke coughed and Juan spat in his cup.

In his effort to show his appreciation, the seaman didn't seem to notice their response.

I exchanged a glance with Hermes who shook his head. He grabbed some of the creamer I like out of the fridge and poured it into the carafe of the heated milk frother. We went about making our breakfast together with gulps and slurps as our soundtrack.

"I have to catch the train," Juan said, rinsing his mug and hanging it. He kissed my son and then gave me a peck on the cheek, clapping Hermes on the shoulder on the way out. "Love you all!"

"I am fond of you as well, human whose name I've forgotten," Cosmo replied in English with oatmeal dripping from his beard.

Juan nodded and let the door shut behind him. His unmitigated laughter trailing in his wake.

"This was ... a hearty meal," the seaman wiped his face with the back of his hand and then inspected the smeared mush. "I will return to my quarters to wash up before I report for duty."

"So, how long before the ISEA agents show up wanting to know about all these gods and whatnot hanging around?" Luke asked after Cosmo left, face grim. "Lucinda is on the Supernatural Council of the Americas and an ambassador to the UN. She has to report their presence."

I stopped stirring my oatmeal long enough to glance at my son. "Good question."

The door creaked open. Lucinda walked in with Arachne. "Forgive me for eavesdropping, but I heard your concern. Milagro Bay is a place for supernaturals. A crossroads most mundanes can't find, so it's neutral ground. That's why ISEA agreed to let you stay here while you learned to use your powers." Her gaze turned to Arachne and then to me. "Gabriel would like to speak to the newcomers so that they understand the rules have changed. Cosmo is the highest admiral in Poseidon's Mighty Eel Navy. That makes the entire council nervous. International waters have no ruler, currently. Gabriel also has concerns about Athena's presence. She has a wide following but needs to understand she cannot influence the current mundane system of government or claim any city on Earth as her own."

Good luck with that, I thought.

The goddess appeared in the doorway, trailed by Nora. "Who is this Gabriel to say what I can or cannot do? I know no deity of that name, only the creature that calls themself an *angel*," she spat the last word as if it were distasteful.

"You're about to find out," Lucinda said, looking at her watch. "The council will be here in a few minutes. By the way, Gabriel is the son of an angel and an indigenous power of this world, a wolf shifter. He and Miriam have grown in power since supes revealed themselves to mundanes. Everyone on the council has, including me. Treat us with the respect you'd give any ruling government of a world, and your stay here will be granted."

I was honestly as shocked as Athena's face expressed.

"Would you speak to Persephone as such?" the goddess asked, hand to chest.

"I have," Lucinda replied. "That's why Spot and I are here, not the queen. Your sibling has made it clear she wishes to reign in Hades, not this world. Hera and your father, Zeus, have sworn to the council their recognition of its sovereignty. You, Athena, were not at the meeting ISEA and the council held. You've made no such oath. Do you understand the concern?"

The goddess switched from shocked to cool and reserved. "I shall hear this Gabriel out, but my business here is for the Oracle's protection, not claiming a city."

Lucinda smiled. It didn't reach her eyes. "Then there should be no problem."

CHAPTER

SEVENTEEN

There was a problem.

The Supernatural Council of the Pacific Northwest sat with Gabriel at one end of my table. Miriam, a white-antlered, pink-haired fae-witch sat to his left. Princess, a black-haired shifter, who wore a leather jacket and a nasty attitude, sat to his right. To her side sat an almost seven-foot-tall willowy blonde, a bigfoot named Aurora. Next to her sat Lucinda.

To Miriam's left, sat a Hawaiian pantheon demigoddess, with eyes, as old and wise as the Earth, set in a pretty, thirty-something face. She had dark curling ringlets and was the only person at the table smiling as she held hands with her Leprechaun husband, Cian. Cian had auburn hair and was shorter than an average-sized mundane human but not as small as the pixies I'd seen in Miriam's faerie.

Behind the council stood an angel and a nephil, and a fae prince named Phyr. I liked Phyr. He'd been nice to me. The angelic rep were a married couple and the enforcers of the council. Shawn, the angel, looked like a movie star. The nephil, Micah, was also model handsome with ginger hair and freckles.

On the other end of my long dining room table sat Athena, Cosmo, and me. Hermes, Arachne, Nicky, Luke, and Cerberus stood behind us. Well, Cerberus lay on the floor next to my feet, but it counted. Nora, a mundane, was not allowed in the meeting. That made me the only person present who didn't look like I could be cast in a fantasy film.

Gabriel had brought a black box the size of a container for wireless ear buds. He'd placed the box on the table. It played a 3D recording of the meeting Athena and I missed. At the meeting, there were representatives of many pantheons, including the Greco-Roman gods. I didn't understand why all of the Twelve weren't there, but then the nature of the meeting came to light. Then I understood why Athena hadn't been invited by her father. If things went south, there would be someone left to rule Olympus.

What kept my focus was the way Apollo whispered in Hera's ear and then Ares. From what I knew, he wasn't buddy, buddy with the two.

We watched the warning from the council and then the warning from the ISEA agents. Agent Roanhorse's acne-scarred face became the focal point of the camera as he ended the meeting with the words, "Whatever disagreements you have between your exterior groups will not be carried out on this world. If we hear otherwise from this council, the International Supernatural Enforcement Agency will make public a fifty-year study about the effects of the power of belief on your kind."

Gabriel clicked the box and the image faded. "Were you aware of this?"

Athena shook her head, her state of distress clear. "I knew of a meeting, but no one told me of this detail."

Hermes put a comforting hand on his sister's shoulder. "The Olympians present at the event have not informed the rest of the warning."

"I'm confused," Cosmo said. "Why is this important?"

Everyone turned toward the seaman, looking confused.

Including me. Even *I* knew that belief affected supernaturals. That's why the angelic anocracy worked with mundane religious leaders to create a zero-tolerance policy about other beliefs. Since this council revealed all myths were based in truth, therefore all magical beings were real, it was a time where mundanes' faith was up for grabs.

"There's a power balance at stake," Gabriel answered.

"We could all fade from existence," Athena whispered. "This is why they want to kill the Oracle. The reason for the attacks on Olympus, Atlantis, and the Underworld. They don't want to rule us all. Whoever is behind the attacks wants to annihilate the competition." She looked at me. "You predicted there would be more shades of gods in Elysian than the living other realms, and the mightiest among us forgotten altogether. I thought you were wrong, but if we don't find out who is doing this, there will be no Olympus or Atlantis, only Hades with a ruler that does not care for any shade."

Fear washed over me like a bucket of icy water sliding over my skin. I had predicted that? No wonder someone used Thetis to try to get rid of me.

"Whatever I saw, it's just one thread," I said, not really believing it myself. It just came out.

"And one interpretation," Hermes added, leaving his sister's back to stand closer to me.

Athena watched his shift in position through narrowed eyes. "The thread the Oracle chooses is always the one that will happen."

"I am a planeswalker," a low voice said from the other side of the room, cutting through the sibling tension.

We all turned our attention to Phyr.

"Not only can I walk from universe to universe, I can travel what you call threads of the fates to the future and the past. There exists a myriad of possible futures. Don't bet on one."

If that was true, the fae was more powerful than I thought.

"Including the one the Oracle saw," Athena answered.

"Yes." The fae responded. "What I'm saying is the threads can splinter and new possibilities occur."

We stared at the fae. Everyone at my end of the table believed that once an Oracle chose a thread, the fates severed all other possibilities. However, was this true?

Miriam cleared her throat and spoke, "Belief is a funny thing. Once a conviction settles in, it's like forged iron, unbendable and very hard to break. The only way to make forged iron bend to a new shape is to go through the fire. That's why cognitive dissonance is so strong in most people. Changing your mind on a core belief, even if that belief is proven wrong, takes enduring pain akin to walking through fire."

"It's painful, but necessary," Gabriel agreed, eyes on Miriam. Then he turned that green-eyed gaze to Athena. "I once thought that everything the Angelic Anocracy taught was true and righteous. The angels had broken away from the teachings of their own creator and started making up rules that suited them. Mundanes did the same thing, persecuting in the name of their religion, conquering and colonizing everything and everyone, using their convictions to oust out every belief but theirs."

They'd sidetracked a bit, but I saw his point. We couldn't be led by what we believed about the Fates.

Gabriel continued, "I think whoever wants to release the Titans and assassinate the other powerful gods wants to follow in those footsteps. They want power and dominion. Because of that, we want to extend the offer of alliance from this council and all who we represent. Whenever that person or persons reveal themselves, we will be there, on your side, Athena."

"Was that foretold?" Phyr asked.

Athena shook her head. "No."

I glanced at Hermes. He also shook his head.

"On behalf of Olympus, I accept the offer," Athena said, "however, our alliance and its purpose must not leave this room. The gods must not know until the traitor or traitors reveal themselves."

EIGHTEEN

A flock of harpies, one siren, a goddess, a god, a Seaman, an Arachne, a mundane priestess, and a slobbery underworld hound congregated in a large gymnasium in the small town of Milagro Bay. It wasn't a high school gymnasium or a gym where you only pumped iron or took a spin class. The facility was like the classical Greek version of a gymnasium that served both as a place for fitness and learning. However, since this was the Pacific Northwest, not classical Greece, the building wasn't marble and open-air.

The harpies had renovated a former warehouse into a state-of-the-art gym visited by the supernatural locals, an arena for martial arts, and classrooms to learn anything from "How to fit in as a mundane when you're not ready to be out as a supe", to the fundamentals of ancient Greek, to knitting circles, or pottery classes.

Nicky owned the facility. It's one of the places where she'd brought Luke to train with the harpies. In ancient times, it would've been set up near the temple, but life wasn't centered around worship anymore, and building up there without supernatural intervention from the gods would be hard and costly.

I'd used the gymnasium's library to learn more about the super-natural world at large—and wow, there was a lot to learn! I also exercised there with Hermes often. However, I hadn't trained as a harpy for two reasons: One, as Oracle for the Gods, using my oracular powers came to the forefront. Two, gaining control of my harpy gifts came second because I hadn't sprouted wings until recently. I also hadn't developed harpy gifts, other than my harpy queen call, which called other harpies to my aid. Screaming for help didn't take training.

However, now that I had wings, I needed to learn to defend myself better than fighting with instincts alone. The battle against Scylla was dumb luck and no skill. There wouldn't be breaks like that again, of that I had little doubt. Training was the best offense against whomever wanted to use me to unlock the gates of Tartarus.

Athena stretched her arms and legs. "Care to spar, brother?"

Hermes bit his lip and glanced at me, indecision holding him back. "I wouldn't deny you, sister, but I was hoping to spar with—"

Nicky stepped between the god and I, cutting him off with a poke to his chest. "Not so fast, Hermes. You may be her partner in every-thing else, but *I* am her mom and a harpy. Go on and spar your sibling. Lydia needs to learn to fight like a harpy queen before she can spar with an Olympian fairly."

Hermes opened his mouth as if to speak, raised a finger, and then shut it firmly.

He must have seen my face when Nicky called herself my mom.

Nicky's declaration served as a balm for a long-suffered heart wound my biological mother left by faking her death and aban-doning me.

"Peace, brother. You have been denied by your lover's kin," Athena said, threading her arm through his. "It never goes well for our kind when we interfere between mother and daughter." As an afterthought, she tossed over her shoulder, "Come, Nora. I wish for you to see this."

The sibling gods went on their way, Nora following her goddess dutifully.

Cosmo turned to Arachne. "Spar?"

The elderly monster eyed the seaman. "Are you sure you're ready for what I've got?"

Cosmo bowed. "I would be honored."

Arachne harrumphed. "Sparring only. Don't get any funny ideas. I know your kind is handsy."

The seaman's thick eyebrows shot up. "I—uh—I would never ... make unwanted advances!"

"The look on your face!" She burst out laughing.

"Oh, you're joking. Ha ha. Very good!'

"Care for a third?" Lucinda asked. "I fight the winner?"

Cosmo nodded.

Arachne grinned. "Never sparred a siren, but I've heard y'all are vicious as harpies. Sure."

"We rarely fight women."

They, too, went on their way to another part of the gymnasium.

Cerberus licked my hand, found a corner, circled three times, and curled up on the floor in his black Labrador form.

I turned to Nicky. "So, what is it today? Swordplay? Hand to hand combat? Grappling?"

Luke chuckled and shook his head. Other harpies laughed, too.

I furrowed my eyebrows and crossed my arms over my chest. "What's so funny? I thought we came here to train. Oh, wait! You're all laughing because it's going to be like one of those action movie training montages where I do seemingly unrelated stuff, like washing and waxing cars. Then when I complain that I want to learn the real moves already, Nicky is going to throw a punch, and I'm going to block it the same way I waxed the car. That's when I'm going to realize you've taught me defensive and lethal combat moves all along."

The harpies either stared, confusion limning their faces, or they whispered to each other, also confused.

"No," Nicky replied straight faced and serious. "We will do training drills to make you strong and agile and teach you to fight."

"We laughed because the question was exactly what your son asked," one of the harpies illuminated.

That made me smile, and it also made me groan internally.

Luke slapped his hand on my shoulder. "You've watched *The Karate Kid* way too many times, ma. I think it did something to your brain."

"Ha. Ha."

"Alright," Nicky barked. "Get in formation."

All of the harpies, including Luke, formed a circle. Nicky urged me to join with a gesture. It felt like P.E. all over again.

Someone put their hand on my right shoulder. Everyone seemed to do the same, so I put a hand on the shoulder of the harpy in front of me. She was taller than me by a good foot, so it was a stretch. "This circle symbolizes that a harpy's strength lies in their community and cooperation within that community. You must act as a cohesive unit. No matter how fast you go, you must make sure that you aren't trampling your neighbor to get there. If your neighbor behind you can't keep up, you must slow your pace so that they don't stumble."

The harpies began a slow jog, and then we were running. I had a hard time keeping up at first, but the harpies adjusted for me. We ran no faster than the slowest person, but I found myself running faster than I would on my own, empowered by the circle.

Next, Nicky had us pair off in twos, keeping me at her side. "Today, you'll observe before we start our lesson."

Some harpies got out bows and arrows from a supply closet and headed outside to the archery range. Luke was among them. Other harpies sparred hand to hand. Some got wooden practice swords. The matches often took to the air.

Strong and agile, the harpies were marvelous to watch. Their screeches weren't shrill and annoying. They were the war cries of women. It was a shame that they were known in popular cultures as vile and repulsive creatures. Then again, men wrote those myths. Why not disarm a powerful woman by making her something unworthy of respect and admiration, let alone love? Not that they needed men at all.

Not all harpies were lesbians, but a good majority of the ones I'd met in Milagro Bay were in a committed relationship with a woman or chose to be single. I bet that rankled ancient mundanes. A whole society of warrior women, who couldn't care less about what a man, or the society men created made of them.

What I saw was weaponized grace. Harpies made fighting as beautiful as a well-choreographed martial arts movie.

"It's time for you to learn flight maneuvers," Nicky said, ripping me from my awe-filled reverie. Her golden wings expanded behind her.

"I can't do that on demand," I protested.

"No problem."

With one hand she clicked a remote with the other she gripped my hand. The domed ceiling opened, like eyelids contracting. She shot straight up without warning.

My stomach flip flopped. A scream tore from my throat.

We were high above the gymnasium, high above the small town of Milagro Bay, the ring of the Olympics in the west and the Cascade Mountains in the far east, the port cities of Washington in the west.

Nicky let go.

At first, I plummeted. Then, instinct took over. My shoulder blades blazed with fiery pain, and then my own wings expanded.

Nicky dove at me.

I evaded. I almost lost control, but my body seemed to know what to do. Kinda like when I tripped, and my body knew to brace for impact or to move my arms to counterbalance.

"Good work!" She shouted. She held up her hands, indicating she wouldn't attack as she flew closer. Nicky smiled as she gave me a midair hug and pulled back. "For someone who hasn't used her wings for most of her life, you have great defensive and evasive instincts."

"Spend over twenty years with a grifter for a spouse, and you too can learn to evade and defend with ease!"

I meant to say it as a joke, but Nicky didn't laugh. She didn't possess a bad sense of humor. Even I could hear the bitterness poison every word, making it not funny at all.

"Your anger with Carlo's betrayal doesn't belong here or anywhere, actually. You must find a way to make peace with what your life has been so that you can have the serenity of mind to face your enemies and enjoy what you have now."

"Yeah. Well, that's not going to happen. I'm not forgiving Carlo. Some people don't deserve forgiveness."

"You're right. Don't forgive him. He doesn't deserve it. That's not what I'm asking. I'm telling you to accept that he was awful, and you'll never get any sort of apology from him. Move on and cherish all the people who cherish and love you."

She gestured to herself and to the gymnasium below. Everything that mattered most was before me and down there: Luke, Hermes, and all my new friends.

Tears, hot and wet, cooled as they slid down my cheeks in the chill air.

I had to let go of not only what Carlo did but what my mother had done. I had to let go of the sense of betrayal and accept that there was nothing I could've done to make them be better people to me. Their priorities had nothing to do with me at all. My worth lay in what I did. Who I was. I didn't need anyone to choose to stay as long as I chose myself.

AFTER THE FIRST day of training, muscles I didn't even know existed yelped. The others, except Luke, seemed unaffected by hours of brutal training and sparring. We got through the family meal together.

Scratch that.

Everyone else got through the meal, I nodded off sitting up, apparently. I had no idea. Waking in Hermes arms would've been sweet if it wasn't because he had to carry me upstairs.

After a nice hot bath drawn by my cinnamon roll of godly boyfriend, I felt more myself.

Hermes waited for me in the bedroom. He massaged my muscles with the expertise of a massage therapist but with the tender care of a lover. I relaxed into his ministrations, letting little moans escape at will. It felt so good, not just physically. I felt how much he cared for me in every stroke.

The concept was foreign to me. My grandparents had been my caregivers when I was a small child, but as they grew aged and infirm, I took on that role. I made the home comfy for Carlos and saw to Luke's needs. I'd spent most of my life caring for others. This treat did not go unappreciated.

It wasn't that I hadn't received massages before.

Thoughts of Carlo giving me massages with the intention of his own gratification floated in. I acknowledged that was the way he was, but it had nothing to do with what was happening now. One day I wouldn't think about Carlo when I received acts of tenderness, and I'd truly be free of him.

"You seem ... different," he mused.

"I've sprouted wings and fought all day."

Got my ass kicked was more like it. If it weren't for my defensive instincts, I would've gotten worse. Nicky hadn't held back. She'd wanted me ready for the next fight, whenever it came.

The handsome god shook his head. "No. There's always this guardedness about you. It's not there now."

I rolled on my side to face him. We were both stark naked, and the sight of his body without clothes did not get old. Once I wiped the metaphorical drool from my mouth, I replied, "I'm making a conscientious choice to let go of the past and enjoy what's before me."

A wicked grin touched his sensuous mouth. "Enjoy how?"

"Any way that I please."

"Oh, yeah?"

"Yeah."

I circled my hand around his length and squeezed. A certain sense of satisfaction rolled through me as he tilted his head back and groaned. Sore and tired as I was, the idea of eliciting more of those sounds from him like that excited me. Besides, I wasn't dead yet, and I had a feeling that we wouldn't get moments like this very often in the near future.

CHAPTER
NINETEEN

The next two weeks involved my new entourage of Athena, Lucinda, and Cosmo; my old crew of Arachne, Hermes, Nicky, Luke, and Cerberus; plus, all the harpies of the local nest going to the gymnasium or coming to the temple with me while I saw petitioners.

Hermes and I only got our nights alone, and I wasn't in any condition to go looking for Hecate then. So, we waited.

Arachne translated my predictions to the petitioners since the Oracle part of me spoke ancient Greek and *I* didn't. Cerberus sat at my feet in his black lab guise. Lucinda and Cosmo flanked my dais on either side.

Between petitioners, Lucinda texted a lot, or made phone calls. She was a mom and had a business to run. I felt guilty the siren had to leave her family just to stand around and do nothing.

There were no attacks upon the temple or the other realms. Hermes traveled back and forth between them as messenger. Zeus wanted daily updates on his brothers.

Athena stayed in the back of the temple, as part of the agreement with the Supernatural Council of the Americas. The goddess would create too much of a stir among mundanes and upset the current balance.

The goddess wasn't alone back there. Nora waited upon her. Athena was also spending the time mentoring the mundane to be one of her priestesses.

Arachne and Athena seemed at an uneasy peace, skirting around each other.

At some point, they would need to work that out.

Today, we set up as usual in the temple. Everyone dressed as if it was a couple thousand years ago in Delphi, or everyday gear in Olympus.

Hermes kissed me goodbye. It was a good kiss, and it reminded me of things he'd done with that mouth the night before. By the look in the god of the crossroads dark eyes, he'd meant to remind me.

"Off with you," I teased.

He grinned. "You can't get rid of me that easily. I'll be back."

After Hermes disappeared into the ether, Cosmo sidled next to me. He smiled, revealing white teeth and dark eyes that crinkled in the corners. "Love is a rare and precious gift. I see it in your eyes when you look at each other, and it makes my heart glad. I am happy for you both, Lydia."

My chest grew tight, and everything around me shrank. Hermes had said he was in love with me, but the very thought of caring that deeply again seemed to knock the world from beneath my feet.

Romantic love never did me any good before. Letting my guard down could place me right back in a situation where I was home waiting to hear the next lie. Love meant watching your best friend grow cold and distant. I would be alone again, the gaping hole in my chest that had started scabbing over the past few weeks ripped wide open again.

Two iron grips squeezed each of my arms. The pain centered me, calling me back from the dark place I was spiraling down to. Cosmo whispered soothing words in a language I didn't understand. Atlantean? I didn't know, but I calmed.

Genuine concern filled the seaman's features. "Where did you go there?"

Good question. I shook my head. I needed to slow things down with Hermes. I let him in much too fast and too easily. "I'm not in love. We're—together, but *I* am not in love."

Cosmo quirked an eyebrow, and then a look of understanding settled on his features. "When you've been hurt, new love can be as terrifying as it is exhilarating. It's wise to let him know why you're not ready to return his sentiment. "

"How do you know so much?" For some reason, I'd imagined seamen living as the stereotype of human sailors with a girl, or guy, in every port.

"I had a wife once. She left me because I—I didn't show her enough affection." He swallowed hard and then rolled his neck as if he could roll out the vulnerability of the confession "I've had quite a few dalliances since. One, I deeply regret not opening myself to. There was nothing wrong with the person. I simply didn't want to feel the pain of letting someone close and to lose everything again. I figured being alone was better than letting her into my life and having her realize I wasn't who she'd hoped I'd be. You see, in my absences while I served, my wife built me up in her head as some hero she wanted me to be rather than who I was. I felt more and more distant from her because I never could live up to the dream. Falling short in someone's eyes again would hurt too much. I should've told her my fears. I should've communicated with my ex-wife that I was imperfect but trying. Don't make my mistake."

I understood that.

Carlo always wanted someone different. Someone more stylish or less demanding than I had been. I spent a lot of time over the years thinking if only I was what he wanted, maybe he wouldn't have cheated. I was afraid that Hermes wanted the idea of me. When I was in harpy form, he couldn't take his eyes off me. I wasn't really the Oracle, even if I was the descendant of a Titan. I'd lived so long as

Madame Francine, the two-bit soothsayer, she was also part of who I was. Would Hermes love her?

I licked my lips. "Were you afraid who you are wasn't good enough?"

Cosmo nodded. "I pushed away a chance of happiness because of my own insecurities. I was afraid the person I was wasn't as good as the admiral who served under Poseidon."

Was I afraid of Hermes leaving or was I afraid of him staying and losing interest in the everyday Lydia Kourakos but not leaving out of some sense of honor or duty? If I was honest with myself, I'd say it was the latter that bothered me more. Either I was or I wasn't good enough and there wasn't anything I could do about it.

"Thank you."

"You're welcome." He grinned, his eyes crinkling in the corners. "I've only known you a short time, but who you are is wonderful, Lydia. I hope you know that."

My cheeks flushed with heat as if I were fifteen again and a cute boy had complimented me. I returned his grin. "So are you."

THE LINE of pilgrims seemed unending. The pilgrims had come from far and wide to hear their future. The Neo-Greco-Roman pagans came from a variety of backgrounds and socioeconomic statuses. Very few of the petitioners were of Greek or Italian heritage, but the Oracle served all who paid alms to the gods.

So many people thought if they only knew what would happen to them, they would have some semblance of control over their lives. I wanted to tell them all to leave, to just live their lives a moment at a time and cherish the good ones. I didn't want to sit on my backside, inhaling noxious fumes and chewing laurel leaves.

I wanted to find Hecate and get full use of my powers. More importantly, I wanted to find out who was trying to start a war among the gods and wanted to use me to do it.

Among the harpies corralling the petitioners outside and at the front of the temple into lines, Luke looked in my direction. At my signal, he ushered the first petitioner to the dais where I sat.

Luke, who liked to lift weights, was a big man. He also had some height to him. However, the petitioner towered next to my son. The man had on the requisite garb, chiton, washed and sandaled feet. He even wore some fresh sprigs of laurel in his curly black hair. Also, there was something about the tall, bearded man that seemed familiar.

Had I seen him before? I was sure I had, but I couldn't place where.

The current influx of pilgrims made it hard to remember faces let alone names. It also had only been two weeks since the fight with Scylla and Charybdis, but whoever caused the trouble was still on my mind.

The petitioner smiled sheepishly and looked around, but there was something about this innocent awe I didn't trust. "Greetings, Oracle."

Cerberus lifted his head, a low growl emitting from his throat.

The stranger held up his hand. "I mean no harm."

I reached for the laurel leaves, but Arachne wasn't there.

Instead of handing me a bowl of laurel leaves, Arachne shut off the artificial stream and then scuttled in front of me before the petitioner reached my tripod stool. She snorted. "You've changed your look, but don't think you can fool me, Nareas."

I smacked my forehead. *Nareas!* That's who he was. How could I forget the daimon who wanted to be a god? A lot had happened, but he should've made a bigger impact. Granted he didn't have a tail and three torsos at the moment. That form wouldn't be easily forgotten.

Lucinda stepped forward as did Cosmo. I had a wall of muscle between me and the daimon.

"I was expecting him," I said to their backs. "Arachne, you know I agreed to decide next full moon. I guess it's been that long."

My guards cleared but remained close.

I stood, facing Nareas, but I didn't speak. I waited to see what he had to say this time.

He smiled, bearing a mouth filled with serrated shark-like teeth. "What say you, Oracle? Do you want my help, or do you want to stay this way?"

I didn't like this daimon. There was something oily about him. Also, I felt like I was bargaining for more than a little statue dedicated to the daimon as a god. I took a stab in the dark. "Let me guess. Your advice is to go to Hecate?"

His eyes widened slightly, but the rest of his face remained in friendly neutrality. If I hadn't been observing people for a long, long time to reveal their tells, I might not have noticed the small shift. However, I had. I was better than average at reading people, and he was at least surprised at my guess.

"No." He shook his head. "I'm not telling you anything until we reach an agreement."

"What agreement?" A cultured feminine voice asked.

We all turned our gazes to Athena. She wore full armor and a helmet, her spear, and her Aegis shield at the ready.

Nareas's smile widened. "I don't think the Oracle wants you to be part of this."

The daimon was right. I didn't.

Athena stepped forward. "I am her guardian. Even against her own bad decisions."

Ouch!

The goddess glanced at me, only long enough that I'd know she was talking to me when she demanded. "Explain why a daimon dares enter this temple."

The old me would've lied through my teeth, but I didn't know if Nareas wasn't part of the larger plot. Also, it was time to let the cat out of the bag, so to speak.

I faced Athena and took a deep breath. "When I make prophecies as the Oracle, I do not have control of my faculties. Nareas spied on me and learned this. Now he's asking for an idol of him to be placed among the gods—" I made a sweeping gesture to indicate the statues of Olympians. "In exchange for the way to maintain control while I'm giving a prophecy."

"I would prefer a cult of my own, but a small altar would do," Nareas said, grinning his shark-toothed smile.

Athena listened, showing no reaction. She didn't reply when he finished. Staring at me yet seemingly through me, the goddess seemed to be thinking. Finally, she spoke, "Something is bound in your soul, segregating your conscious mind and your Oracle gift. Nareas doesn't know how to fix the problem, but I'm sure your guess is correct. Hecate is the mother of magic and witchcraft. She would know how to break whatever spell was cast upon you."

It had been Hermes's guess, actually, but I didn't say that out loud.

Nareas licked his lips and rubbed his hands together. "Ah, but do you know where Hecate is?"

Athena's eyes flared, anger hardening every feature. She switched to Greek when she said, "You do not deserve to be among us, daimon. You seek humans to serve you, to give you power, but once you become a god, you serve them." She pointed her spear at the idols. "Go ahead, have an altar here. See what it is to be molded by them, to have your very existence shaped by their imagination like clay to be sculpted." She added in a barely audible whisper, "Or neglected."

I recalled on our road trip out here Hermes telling Cerberus that none of them were what they once had been. She possessed a city dedicated to her name, she had been the protector of Athens, but the inhabitants had turned to other gods.

"You all are my witnesses. The goddess Athena gave me permission." Nareas laughed, a note of victory echoing in the sound. His shit-eating grin doubled and tripled as three heads sprang from his body. His torso blurred and became three as well. Two legs coalesced into a long tail. "I will commission a sculptor as soon as possible."

His body faded until all that were left were three smiles, like Cheshire Cat triplets, and then nothing.

"Nareas was a minor daimon. How can he still exist?" Athena asked no one and everyone at once. Her gaze remained on where the daimon had stood.

Arachne cleared her throat, but her voice still sounded softer than usual when she replied, "He might have been like most, clinging to life but without much power. Athens opened an Acropolis Museum a little over ten years ago. A statue of him is featured there. It's nameless, but likely all he needed to regain some power."

Athena turned to her former friend. "Perhaps you could tell me more about this world and how it has changed? Nora can perform your duties while we speak." The goddess extended her hand.

Arachne gave me a cursory glance.

I couldn't nod hard enough in approval. We watched the two join hands, returning to the back. My chest ached for Arachne's heartbreak she'd held on to for so long. I hoped this would lead to a true reconciliation between the two of them.

TWENTY

We sat around the dinner table, debating who would make the trip to the Underworld and who wouldn't. Hermes was in. Athena was in. Cerberus was in because it was the pooch's home turf. Cosmo and Lucinda were in because they were assigned as protectors, and that should've been enough, but Luke and Nicky had other ideas. Thankfully, Arachne kept her peace. Nora and Juan, the mundanes among us unable to make the trip, tried to eat their dinner in peace.

I felt for them, and I felt for me.

I didn't want to go to Hades and look for a witch goddess who might or might not be able to fix me. I didn't want so many people with me, and for the past week or so, Luke was stepping so far into this world, he might get as lost in it as I am.

Nora and Arachne began clearing the table while the rest argued on. Nicky was pointing out how harpies were more welcome than Olympians in the Underworld. Luke, who'd never left this world, was adamantly backing his grandmother—because she was making his case.

Juan got up. The argument raged on as if he didn't exist. We met gazes. He shook his head, hurt in his eyes before he quietly left the room. The sojourn into the supernatural was supposed to be temporary for my son. He'd swore to Juan they'd go back to their life and that he wanted nothing to do with this one.

"Luke."

He didn't hear me, or at least acted like he couldn't. I had harpy hearing now. It was a lot sharper than my middle-aged ears could hear before I sprouted wings. I knew his young ears had to have benefited too.

I tried once more. "Luke."

"Lucas Kourakos, I am speaking to you." I threw all the motherly sternness I could muster into the sentence.

It worked. A little too well, actually. Everyone stopped talking and faced me.

"Juanito left, and you didn't even notice."

Luke glanced at the empty spot where Juan had sat. He brushed it off with a wave of his hand. "He's fine."

"I don't agree. Maybe you should go check on him?"

Luke gave me a hard stare. "He went upstairs because he was done eating, ma. Don't meddle in my relationship."

"She wasn't meddling. I think your mother was saying—" Hermes began.

Luke turned a glacial glare on my boyfriend. "Look, you're cool and all, and I'm glad you're making my ma happy, but you're not my pops. So don't try to do what you're doing."

The god held up his hands in mock surrender.

I reared my head in shock that Luke would speak this way to me or anyone. "Meddle? Meddle? I've never said a word about any of your relationships except to support you. Who is this meddling mother?"

Luke wiped a hand over his face. "Ma, leave it."

"All I'm saying is that Juan looked upset and that you should check on him before committing to an adventure."

"The matter of this expedition is more important than a lover's quarrel. Let the kids figure it out, Lydia," Nicky advised as if she'd been my stepmother all along.

Sick of so many eyes and opinions, I asked my son, "Can we speak in private for a moment?"

Luke blew out his breath and nodded.

We headed to the kitchen, standing at opposite ends. "Please consider not going, Luke. It's dangerous, and your involvement in the supernatural world is temporary. It's not worth risking your life, let alone the strain on your relationship."

Luke plopped onto a kitchen chair. "All my life, you've protected me and sheltered me from dad's grifting and your life. I always felt like I was missing a big piece of who you and dad were. I didn't know my grandparents or any of either of your relatives for that matter. For the first time, I feel like I'm part of a family, something bigger. Let me have this, ma."

I knew the feeling, however— "Juan has been your family longer than anyone here, but me. I think if you go with us, you might be risking a good thing, maybe the best thing."

My son rested his face in his hands. "I feel like you're not listening."

I scoffed and crossed my arms. "Funny. I could say the same."

Our reunion honeymoon was over. We'd been so happy to be back in each other's company that we behaved as politely as strangers. Now we had lived under the same roof for a few months, old dynamics set in. Except, Luke wasn't a teenager to be scolded anymore.

He pressed the heels of his palms into his eyes.

My heart ached. Luke did that when he really didn't want to cry, but the tears were coming anyway. He did that when he told me and Carlo that he needed gender affirming care, and Carlo wouldn't listen. I could've lost him then if I hadn't saved up and took him to specialists. This felt that serious.

I unfolded my arms and approached my son, putting a hand on

his shoulder. "I'm sorry it feels that way. My actions came from a place of caring for you both and wishing I'd had the same love as you two have. This is your life, and you must live it the way you see fit."

"I don't want to go back to my old life, working some job as a software guy and pretending I'm nothing special, ma. I am."

My stomach balled into a knot of dread, fearing what I knew he'd say next.

"Don't get me wrong, I like what I do, but I want to be part of this family, part of the supernatural community. I want to stay in Milagro Bay and live as a harpy." Luke lifted his head. His eyes were red and puffy. "That's why Juan is upset. He sees no place for him here."

So far, no one, but Arachne, Nicky, Hermes and I knew he had the potential of being an Oracle. If Luke stayed here, he'd assume the risk of that circle widening. Then again, if he left, he wouldn't be under the protection Milagro Bay and the harpies afforded. Either way, I couldn't keep my son safe. That was the most basic of parental responsibilities.

"Since you know what you're risking, I have no more advice," was all I could manage to say.

Hermes stood in the doorway. "I'm sorry to interrupt. We're going to vote on who comes. It's the only way to end the debate."

Luke rose and left.

The god let my son through but waited for me, taking me in his arms and holding me. I could feel how much Hermes loved me. I cared for him, but part of me screamed not to give as much as he gave me. It wasn't fair, but neither were the things that had happened to me. The nice thing about being immortal was that I'd have time to recover and learn to trust my heart to him. I only hoped two things: we'd survive the storm ahead, and Hermes wouldn't decide I wasn't worth semirequited feelings and leave me.

~

THE VOTE WAS BRUTAL. Everyone wanted Nicky, she was a seasoned harpy, knew the Underworld better than Lucinda, and could communicate better than Cerberus. Luke's new family decided he didn't have the skills to join on this journey. He didn't take it well.

I let Nicky follow and console him. He was still sore with me for calling him out about Juan and probably blamed me for the vote.

Lesson learned. Mind my business when it came to my son's relationships.

The dinner broke up after that so we could all get some rest. Arachne, Nora, and Luke would go to the temple in the morning to light a special fire that would release red smoke, signaling I wasn't there. Hopefully, that would keep Luke from wallowing in his room because he couldn't come with us.

Hermes followed me to my room. He'd abandoned his since the first night we made love. However, he still asked, "May I keep you company?"

The fact that he asked, that he didn't assume sex or even my personal space wasn't guaranteed warmed my heart in ways he would never know. "I'm tired and frayed. Would you be satisfied with spooning?"

The corner of his mouth quirked. Amusement danced in his eyes. "Spooning?"

I chuckled and then explained, "You hold me, or I hold you in bed like two spoons in a drawer."

"I would love to fork you, but spooning sounds nice."

"Oh, that pun was so terrible it was good." Laughing, I opened the door.

He snaked an arm around my waist as we entered, and whispered against my nape, "I'm the big spoon."

I wiggled against him. "Another dirty pun? You naughty god."

His voice lowered a few octaves when he replied, "You have no idea."

"I have some idea."

"You've had a sample." He shut and locked the door behind him. "I don't want to reveal all my ... *gifts* at once, but I shall reveal them."

Something in that promise made me want to do more than spoon. However, once we readied for bed and got under the covers, I surrendered to sleep—warm and safe in Hermes's arms.

TWENTY-ONE

Shades drifted past. Some were more solid than others. None seemed to see us, lost in their memories, so it seemed. My attention wasn't really on them. I kept my gaze on the glittering ever-night firmament. There, Lucinda flew so high I could barely see her from the party's vantage point in the field of asphodel. She neared fast, descending and landing right in front of us within moments.

Lucinda was a pretty lady. However, in siren form, she was magnificent. Her wings were rainbow hued and iridescent. Colorful feathers matching her wings covered her body. Her fingers and toes were sharp talons that appeared to be metallic. Her eyes glowed electric blue. The lights in her eyes dimmed to a rich brown. The feathers molted and turned to glittery dust. Her hands and feet were once more human.

I offered her the boots she'd left behind.

She sat to put them on, talking as she dressed. "My queen doesn't know where Hecate has hidden herself away and advises us to seek the judges. One of them is surely aware of where the goddess sleeps."

I blew my breath out my nostrils. Of course, we'd have to seek out someone else to guide us. Of course, it wasn't one person we'd have to search out, but a possibility out of three. Because I grew up on Greek myths, I knew things worked in threes, but part of me had wanted Persephone to reply, *"Oh yeah, my old pal Hecate is hiding out in a cabin in Elysium. I'll draw you a map."*

At least there were only three: Rhadamanthus, Minos, and Aeacas. Here's to hoping that the three judges, or Hecate herself, didn't send me on twelve labors. I had a lot going on and wasn't in the mood for a Herculean task.

"Which should we seek first, sister?" Hermes asked Athena.

The goddess seemed to ponder the question for a bit before replying. "I leave that decision to you, brother. You are the one who guides the shades to their judgement."

Hermes scratched the back of his head. A playful smile touched his lips. "I may have made Thanatos believe that father wanted him to take over the position."

Athena touched her chest. Offended didn't cover the expression coloring her face. Mortally wounded might be a more apt description. I'm pretty sure Athena was a rule follower and Hermes bent and broke them whenever possible. Hermes and I shared that personality trait.

"You did not shirk the sacred responsibility of psychopomp!"

The god shrugged. "The job gets done. Thanatos likes dealing with the dead, anyway. It's his thing."

Her nostrils flared, and she pinched her lips so tight, they went bloodless.

Everyone gathered backed up a step or six. No one was willing to get caught in the godly sibling battle crossfire, including me.

"Oh, sister, there were fewer shades coming in after the treaty with the Angelic Anocracy. It gave Thanatos something to do." He glanced around and forced a shudder. "Quite honestly, our sister Persephone's domain gives me the creeps. It's spooky."

Athena quirked an eyebrow. "Spooky?"

He nodded, straight faced. "Very much so. It's dark and foreboding."

We stood in a beautiful field of flowers under a perpetual twilight. The palace in the distance had a gothic aesthetic, but this realm seemed peaceful and kind to me.

The goddess shook her head and heaved an exasperated sigh. "Eons old and still a child." She then turned her gaze to me. "How do you, a practical and wise woman, allow such a fool in your bed is anyone's guess."

His eyebrows lowered, and he narrowed his eyes. *That* hit a nerve. "Perhaps because I'm rather handsome and charming. Likable. Don't worry about where I sleep. Instead, wonder why you have been without a companion for far too long, sister."

The goddess of wisdom's eyes glowed as Athena sputtered.

Cerberus whined.

"So which judge should we visit first?" I asked, putting myself physically between them in order to stop the argument before it reduced to hair pulling and lightning bolts zinging around.

"Rhadamanthus's keep is the closest to where we are now," Lucinda offered, drawing closer.

When the siblings started squabbling, everyone had backed up. Well, except Cerberus, who sat dutifully at my feet all three heads panting and anxiously awaiting. I gave the pooch a reassuring pat.

"We could walk to Styx from here and take the ferry there," Nicky added. The wall between siblings grew as she sidled next to me. Cosmo followed suit on the other side.

Hermes waved his hand dismissively. "Everywhere is close when you're with the God of the Roads. We should puzzle out which one Hecate would trust the most."

Athena scoffed. Then she murmured, "Puzzle out. You would know if you'd been doing your duty as psychopomp instead of creating grandiose titles, you would know where Hecate is."

"I say we go to Rhadamanthus," I said a little too loudly and smiled too brightly at Hermes, hoping to distract him. "Either he knows, or he doesn't."

Cerberus's three heads barked their agreement. Or at least I'd like to believe the Underworld guard dog was agreeing with me and he wasn't just excited to play and roam.

"If you wish to go to Rhadamanthus, then I will take you there," Hermes vowed. He shot a glance at his sister, adding, "As my non-made-up title of God of the Roads, I can take you anywhere."

"I do."

The group gathered around Hermes as he led the way through the cold interstitial space between universes. The trip took only a few seconds, but my entire body shivered uncontrollably by the time we reached Rhadamanthus's keep.

Hermes swept me in his arms and rubbed my back. Concern was etched on the sculpted angles of his face, as he peered down at me. "As soon as you signed the contract to be the Oracle, you should've been able to tolerate the roads between worlds."

He kept his voice low, which I appreciated.

However, everyone around noticed the effect crossing had on me. Cerberus licked my hand. Nicky looked on with the same expression I imagine I had when Luke wasn't feeling well. Athena's brow furrowed in concern. Cosmo had reached for me when we first crossed but retracted his hand, thinking better of it, when Hermes glared.

"Perhaps if you traveled in your harpy form, you'll not feel the effects?" Nicky suggested.

I doubted it mattered, but I tried anyway.

She was right. The shaking stopped, and we were able to resume our course to the keep of Rhadamanthus.

Ahead, a curved wall several stories high was topped by several rounded walls, each tier smaller than the one below. The stories and the outer wall were all white. Except for the bottom wall, which remained smooth and flawless, open windows dotted the tiers. The tops of the windows were arches, and deep, purple vines with bright pink flowers spilled from the bottom sill of the window. The effect looked like a white cake with pretty decorations, not a foreboding keep.

I craned my head, taking it all in. "Why does the judge need a keep in the middle of Hades? It's the land of the dead. Not many invading forces looking to take over his land, I'd imagine."

"Shades aren't the only inhabitants of Hades," Athena replied, her gesture sweeping to Cerberus, Nicky, and Lucinda.

Right. Not all sirens and harpies lived on my world. Besides them, my grandparents had told me stories about the monsters who lurked here. I shivered, but it wasn't from the crossing this time.

There seemed to be no way in. "Do we need to walk around to the gate?"

As if in response, a horn blared, and a portion of the white wall dissolved into an iron portcullis. The portcullis raised. I expected some sort of retinue since we weren't, well, expected.

Instead, a singular, black-robed figure with their face obscured by the shadows of a hood waited. Folded wings the same purple as the vines rested on the stranger's back. A thin-fingered hand with grayish skin, the only visible body part of our greeter, held a scythe.

Hermes gripped my hand, positioning himself slightly in front of me.

A raspy voice called, "Hermes, you lying scoundrel! How dare you show up here? Especially now."

I sighed inwardly.

This was just what we needed.

A pissed off Angel of Death.

CHAPTER

TWENTY-TWO

"Seems as though Thanatos doesn't like your trickery, brother. Hold your tongue and let me settle this," Athena muttered low enough that if I didn't have my harpy hearing, I wouldn't have heard her. Then she took a step forward, assuming the role of leader. Loud enough so that the angel could hear, the goddess said, "Your quarrel with Hermes will have to wait. He's been assigned by the three God-kings to perform a duty. If you interfere, you'll have to answer to me and then my father and his brothers."

"Oh, Athena. Still defending little brother even when he doesn't deserve it, I see." A laugh that sounded akin to rustling leaves escaped the hood.

Thanatos's laughter was met with an icy stare from the goddess. The rest of us didn't find his teasing amusing either, most of all, me. I didn't like he had a beef with Hermes or that he chose this confrontation now. We had Hecate to find, my powers to unbind, and a plot to unravel.

Thanatos held up his free hand. "Alright, alright. Tough crowd. I'll deal with Hermes later. What business do you have here?"

"We came to see Rhadamanthus," I replied.

125

"Funny that. So did I. He hasn't shown up to the court of judgment for a while now, and the souls waiting to become shades there are accumulating. Looks like all of Rhadamanthus's staff haven't seen him since the last breach of the gates of Tartarus. We had all hands on deck with that one, yet nobody saw what happened to him."

My stomach dropped. My company exchanged glances. Everyone seemed at unease with the answer. Likely because, unless you were a younger god like Hermes, you didn't just stop doing a sacred duty or pawn it off to someone else. His disappearance wasn't random.

Athena spoke first, "Why haven't Minos and Aeacus simply carried on with judgements in his absence? They don't need him."

That wasn't the question that burned in my mind, I wanted to know where Rhadamanthus went, but Athena had a point.

Thanatos shook his hooded head. "Also, a funny story, but not funny ha ha, but funny weird. They're missing too, I'm afraid."

"I have to report to the palace. My queen must hear of this," Lucinda insisted.

Nicky gave me an apologetic look. "King Aidoneus will want a report, too."

Thanatos held up a bony hand. "Hold your wings, ladies. Hades is the one who sent me. He already knows about Minos and Aeacus. I'm the one he wants to hear from about Rhadamanthus."

Lucinda stepped forward. "That can't be true. My queen sent me to seek out the three judges."

My dropped stomach twisted into a knot of leaden worry. It couldn't be good that there was a breach in the gates of Tartarus, a battle was fought, and the rulers of Hades weren't communicating.

"So, if you weren't looking for Rhadamanthus for the three God-kings, what did you want with him?" Thanatos somehow conveyed he was speaking to Athena without being able to see his face let alone where he looked.

"I'm looking for Hecate. I need her help," I responded for her.

Thanatos laughed again. "Persephone knew Hermes wouldn't be

too keen on looking for me and might have tried to seek out Hecate without asking for my help, so she sent you to where I might be. Clever goddess."

The assessment didn't place Hermes in the best light, but I didn't have exactly the best track record either. I used to con people out of their money, pretending I could see the future. We were more of a matched pair than I realized.

"You know where Hecate rests?"

"I do." Thanatos replied. "Unfortunately, she's in a place where I would have to lead you, and I must find these judges. How about you help me and then I show you?"

Hermes looked at me. "I know my opinion is likely not as valued as before you knew my secrets, but I think that we should continue to try ourselves."

He had a point. I really, really didn't want to go on a side quest.

"Brother, the missing judges may have something to do with the plot that could cost your love her life," Athena warned.

She had a point, too.

Cerberus whined, relating exactly how I felt. Part of me wanted to uncover who was conspiring against the gods and wanted me to do it. The other part wanted to find Hecate and not embark on a side quest.

Hermes blew out his breath and then grinned at his sibling. "Presenting us with an answer which is a riddle to solve is Persephone's way of leading us to get both tasks accomplished without assigning them."

"True. I appreciate our sister not using her position to outright boss us around like when she was a child."

The siblings shared a look that seemed like a whole conversation without words and a grin. Whatever squabble they had earlier forgotten.

I felt happy for them, truly. But the memories they shared created mixed feelings that weren't envy yet was completely envy. I didn't grow up with brothers and sisters nor did I have anyone left to share memories with from my childhood. My grandparents had been wonderful, but elderly. They'd died before I'd finished growing up, leaving me alone to fend for myself.

Though I didn't begrudge them, my chest ached for a past I didn't have. A sister like Athena around would've kept Carlo away. At least I could console myself that I had Luke from that union, and since have added to the people who cared about me.

A strange sound akin to clearing a throat, if that throat was made of bone and stone, took me out of my thoughts. The sound came from Thanatos. "I hate to interrupt your trip down memory lane, but I have judges to find."

"We shall join you," Athena answered for us all.

TWENTY-THREE

"I don't like this," Lucinda confessed in a whisper. "It doesn't make sense. My queen wouldn't have sent us to the three judges if she knew any of them were missing."

I nodded in agreement. It felt like we were going in circles. However, I recalled that was the way many Greek epics went. The heroes did indeed go in circles. Was that a good sign, or was I only repeating history?

We approached the palace, led by a siren and a harpy to the same den where I'd spoken with Persephone alone before. We were urged to make ourselves comfortable, but no one sat. Athena drew Hermes and Thanatos to the corner of the room. The three spoke in low tones. Guess you had to be a god or a personification of death to get in that circle.

It chaffed to be a secondary figure in all of this when we were supposed to be here to find Hecate and get my oracular stuff together.

The king and queen of the underworld arrived together, arms linked and faces somber. They wore simple black peplos and himations wrapped around their shoulders that looked as if they were spun of the eternal twilight firmament of their realm. Each wore an onyx crown. They may have met us in their den, but their vestments seemed to symbolize they were here in their official capacity.

Persephone's gaze darted among those gathered, settling the longest on her siren general. Her expression revealed nothing.

"According to the servants, the three judges and their retinue did not return after the battle," Thanatos declared.

King Aidoneus Hades's throat bobbed as he swallowed hard, his only show of emotion. "Thank you for confirming, Thanatos."

The personification of Death waved a bony hand. "Shall I pursue them?"

The god of the underworld shook his head slowly. A mournful sigh escaped his lips. "That won't be necessary. I had to make sure they didn't take refuge in their keeps. You can avoid a king and queen, but you can't avoid Death."

"Now, that we know they didn't return," Persephone added, "we can be sure of where they were taken."

Aidoneus smiled bitterly. "Or, where they went of their own accord."

Tension blanketed the room as we waited for the queen or ancient king to elaborate.

A knock broke the silence.

"Enter," Persephone called.

Two siren soldiers marched in. They bowed to their queen, ignoring everyone else present.

"Report."

"The judges' retinues were all found on the shore of the River Lethe. None recall how they got there, let alone where the judges were taken."

A siren could get anyone to tell the truth let alone their deepest darkest secrets.

"Let them return home. Assign a unit to shadow them at each keep. The effects of the Lethe are not always permanent," Persephone ordered. "Also, there's a possibility whomever got them to drink will be back to do it again."

The sirens bowed to their queen, also lowering their heads to Lucinda on the way out. She must rank very high in Persephone's forces to get that sort of acknowledgement when no one else got a second glance.

Once the sirens left, Aidoneus turned his attention to all of us. "Those soldiers were loyal to Whomever did this and wanted to discredit me and my wife's ability to rule this realm. The attack was subterfuge, not an actual attempt of Titans to break free. The ones we didn't thwart retreated to Tartarus. Once you break free of a place like that, you'd only return if you believed it would be short lived. I'm sure they took the judges there. They'll prove valuable, if the gods are overthrown and there are many dead mortals to judge."

"Do you think they took Hecate, too?" I asked. I knew before I received several dark looks that it was the wrong time to ask, but I needed to know.

"My dear friend would not be taken by anyone," Aidoneus said, a glimmer of a smile touching the god's lips.

Persephone nodded her agreement and added, "However, she is very old and cranky. She's likely sleeping somewhere, protected by her descendants. She never says where she's going to us, but usually tells one of the judges where she rests because they don't care enough to tell anyone."

That was odd. They talked about a powerful Titan as if she were a quirky grandmother. Then again, Arachne fit that bill, too. Thanatos seemed to be a smartass with an absurd sense of humor as well. Some scary immortal beings they all were.

Thanatos sighed, a gravelly sound. "Sometimes Hecate tells me where she's going for the same reason."

"This time?" Athena asked, trembling with rage.

"Yup."

"You could've told us sooner!" she shouted, voicing everyone else's thoughts.

Unfazed by her wrath, Thanatos shrugged. "By conning me into being the psychopomp, Mr. Trickster has made my life hard for—oh, about four or five thousand mortal lifetimes. Do you have any idea how many souls that is? I was going to tell you all, but I could see he really wanted it. I wasn't going to give him *anything* he wanted that easily."

I bit my lip so I wouldn't scream. There were machinations afoot, and Thanatos thought he'd bring us all on a wild goose chase, knowing the location of Hecate the whole time to pay Hermes back for a prank pulled thousands of years ago. Children! All of these immortals were children!

I exchanged a glance with Lucinda. No wonder she chose to leave Persephone's army and be an ambassador. I would've used any excuse to have gotten away from a realm filled with bored immortals as fast as I could too.

However, no one was looking at Thanatos too kindly right now.

"The Oracle needs Hecate to prevent this war," Persephone said through her teeth.

The angel of death held up his bony hands. "Okay. Okay. In hindsight, I could've picked a better payback." He turned to me. "I'll take you, but really, you need better taste in men."

Everybody's a comedian. Even Death.

CHAPTER

TWENTY-FOUR

I thought Thanatos would lead us to somewhere in the underworld, instead we ended up in a small trailer park on top of a hill. The community wasn't like the rundown ones I'd seen in movies and on the East Coast. No cars with the engine on the lawn or appliances on the patios. Though some of the mobile homes were the old metallic kind, they were well taken care of, so much so, they appeared brand new. The rest were double-wides with expensive-to-me vehicles parked in the driveways. Well-loved old growth gardens of flowers and other pretty shrubbery decorated the yards. Evergreens dotted the landscape, between which lay an incredible view of forested hills, the dark waters of the Puget Sound, and the Olympics on one side and the Cascade Mountains in the far distance on the other. The few residents milling about their lawns or picking up mail from a communal mail locker, didn't look younger than seventy. However, there was something about them that seemed unlike regular retirees.

After walking a bit, I put a finger on what it was. They didn't have the posture or walk of an elderly person. Like Zeus and Poseidon, the residents had the façade of age, but none of the tell-tale signs of a body breaking down after a mortal lifespan of use.

Must be nice.

I was getting in better shape, rapidly, but I felt every single workout. If it weren't for my excellent tub, Epsom salts, ibuprofen, and Hermes's magic hands, I'd likely feel worse. Technically, I'd never age any more either, so I couldn't be too envious.

What was stranger than their lack of aging was that they paid us no mind. They walked about as if Thanatos in his dark robes carrying a scythe, Athena and Hermes, a siren, a harpy, a seaman, a woman with a three headed dog that didn't bother to take on his black Lab guise were an everyday occurrence.

We followed Thanatos to a double-wide with all sorts of green and growing things. Even more verdant than the rest. A woman in a broad brimmed hat and a flannel shirt under overalls tucked into rubber boots with a ladybug pattern pruned her hedges with long pruning shears. She stopped her work and turned to face us. Her features were quite beautiful in an ageless face. The strands of hair that escaped the hat were silver and black, and curly like mine.

"Himalayan blackberries are the worst! They grow up to ten feet tall, and the vines can stretch forty feet long. They grow so thick that all the plants native to the area have no chance. Wildlife can't get through the thick of them. If I were to lock a person away in a shed never to be found, all I'd have to do is put a few around the building and within a year there would be no reaching them."

Thanatos's raspy chuckle the only reaction that wasn't confusion from our group. "Hecate, be careful. We have a representative from the Supernatural Council of the Americas with us. She might revoke your visa."

Hecate's dark eyes narrowed on the siren. "Are you a snitch for ISEA?" She'd pronounced the agency "I see." However, it was safe to assume she meant the International Supernatural Enforcement Agency.

Lucinda shrugged. "I'm not responsible for visas, and I avoid

ISEA as much as possible."

The woman laughed. "Good answer, ambassador. What brings the lot of you here to an old lady?"

I stepped forward. For once, I'd like to speak for myself, do something I decided to do. "My name is Lydia Kourakos. I'm the current Oracle, but the oracular part of me is ... segregated from my conscious mind. Would you be able to help?"

Hecate stared at me. Her eyes bored through me as if she were dissecting my very soul. The world around us stilled. The white noise of a community: the wildlife, the people, the cars, the gazillion things that hummed and whirred silenced. Suddenly, all the noise and motion returned. The goddess removed her garden gloves and stuffed them in the front pocket of her overalls.

"Come on in and let me get cleaned up a bit. I think I know what your problem might be."

THE GODDESS'S double-wide was too small for the entire party, so Cerberus, Lucinda, Nicky, and Cosmo remained outside. I wished she'd disinvite Thanatos. Something about the guy got on my nerves. Perhaps I wasn't over the wild goose chase he'd led us on. I was also perturbed with Persephone for not telling us about the judges. Despite her stopping my train on my way out here to take me to meet the shade of my mother, the Queen of the Underworld hadn't been on the lists of "Gods Who Waste My Time Just Because They Can" but given a chance, she'd gotten herself added to the list.

The interior of the double-wide had the appearance of a turn-of-the-century cabin. Drying herbs and flowers hung in the modest kitchen, giving the place a fabulous aroma. Hecate pointed to the living space. The red velvet upholstery of a couple of antique chairs, a loveseat, and a full-sized sofa all matched. A beautifully woven rug, reminiscent of my grandmother's work, covered most of the floor of the living space.

I took a seat on the loveseat, and Hermes sat next to me. Thanatos took a chair as did Athena.

Hecate disappeared into the back to wash up and returned, wearing a powder blue peplos with a gold belt, gold earrings, necklace, and bracelet. Gold laurel leaf hair pins replaced the wide-brimmed hat on her salt and pepper curls.

The difference in Hecate's appearance was striking.

I wished my wardrobe changes had such dramatic effect. Then again, I wasn't an ancient goddess. For all I knew, it was magical smoke and mirrors. Still, I'd give credit where credit was due.

"You look fantastic."

"I know." She grinned. Then she was all business, moving the coffee table to the kitchen with a twitch of her nose. A flick of her wrist and a sheet with unfamiliar markings floated out of the back and settled on the floor.

I wanted to remark that she reminded me of Samantha from *Bewitched*, but Hecate had been around a lot longer than televisions existed. With an elegant sweep of her hand, she indicated for me to lie down on the sheet.

As I settled down, I looked in Hermes's direction. I saw something I hadn't before. His jaw was tight, and his eyes were hard. Every inch of him seemed coiled with tension as if he was readying himself to spring to my defense.

Hecate's gaze followed mine. She laughed. "Stop looking at me as if I'm going to scoop out her eyeballs. I won't harm the Oracle. We haven't anymore left to replace her with."

The last statement wasn't reassuring.

"It's not like she's completely defenseless. The Oracle defeated a Titan all on her own," Athena began and then warned in a mock-chastising tone, "If you cannot calm yourself, brother, perhaps you should wait outside."

Their teasing only seemed to strengthen his resolve to be an overprotective grumble butt.

"I'm staying with Lydia," he declared.

I had to admit. Annoying as growly men were, I thought it was sweet. Especially since he said my name, not "the Oracle." When Hermes met my gaze, I smiled at him. Without knowing how this would turn out, I couldn't offer more in the way of reassurance, but it seemed to be enough.

The god's dark eyes softened in response.

Hecate sat cross-legged, her leg brushing the top of my head. She placed her hands on either side of my face, fingertips pressed to my temples.

A shock that was a lot more than static electricity shot through me.

"Wait!"

The goddess removed her hands. "What is it?"

"What are you going to do?"

"You have a complex spell woven into your soul. I was going to untangle it and remove it."

"Oh." I said stupidly. Then I had more questions. "Will it hurt?'

"Yes. Immensely." Her gaze flicked to Hermes. "You interfere, and it will kill her, maybe me, and I'd be very put out if I became a shade."

I grinned. I couldn't help myself. Using humor to deflect a serious situation was my go-to, and she made a *Princess Bride* reference. I was sure it was meant for me.

"Ready, Lydia?"

I nodded and closed my eyes. Somehow, I thought it would be better that way. I was wrong.

Hecate was not kidding about the pain.

I screamed in agony. Every cell in my body burst one by one. As the rest of me went *snap* and *pop,* someone was trying to soothe me with words. My brain couldn't glean any meaning from the sounds. The only physically grounding outside of the pain was Hecate's firm grip on my head. Then that too was lost. I drowned in the pain until the corners of my waking mind folded into the void.

CHAPTER
TWENTY-FIVE

A myriad of voices rang in my head. Showing me their lives, our lives. The Oracle family tree spread out and branched before me. I could pluck a life and absorb every moment as easily as I could pluck an apple and eat it.

Through these lives, I learned our story.

We were first the progeny of Zeus and Dione, in Dodona. Then their descendants and Zeus. He grew bored of us. He was king of the gods, and no future we could see interested him. Some of us made our way to Delphi, where we were protected by the dragon-serpent Python.

Then came Apollo. He killed Python, our protector, and told us that he was our protector now. Protection came with serving him as we had Zeus. The ichor of the two gods flowed in our children's veins. We prospered, and so did our people.

Then the wars came. Wars of men and wars of gods. Even in our mountain refuge, new ideas sprang. No one sought us for the future. Instead of being revered, we had to hide what we were.

Apollo grew bored. Dione abandoned us. Our daughters forgot

our ways, became Christians. Served a singular god with many saints. Their power diminished.

A revival. The people no longer worshipped the gods of Olympus, but they placed our items of worship in museums. They preserved what was left of our temples. Some though, began to worship the old gods in secret.

Dione returned to us, choosing one girl, training her, and then we served in secret. Apollo no longer wanted anything to do with an Oracle whose ichor was too weakened by mortal blood to be of use. Hermes became our protector. Unlike Zeus and Apollo, he didn't ask us to serve him in the way we'd served his father and brother. Except our blood needed his strength.

On the tree, I saw Apollonia's life. Her life and magic shone more brightly. Her magic was stronger than the line had been in thousands of years.

My soul or spirit trembled as I peered inside my mother's life.

I ran down the hill. A fresh breeze blowing my hair from my face. My heart raced in my ears. I wouldn't let a boy catch me. I could see my village. Once there, he wouldn't dare touch me.

My toe caught on something. I stumbled forward, tumbling head over heels. I rolled over rocks, sticks, and sheep's dung. Finally, my body lost momentum.

Embarrassed, filthy, and hurt, I cried.

"There, there, my darling. We all fall down. The important thing is that we get back up." My mother extended one of her graceful hands to me.

I put my small hand into hers, letting the warmth pass from the long, elegant fingers into me. The dull throbbing in my head went away as well as the burning scratches and dull aches.

We smiled at each other as I rose. "Thank you, mama."

We strolled to our home, hand in hand. The boy and the tumble forgotten. He wouldn't chase me with my mother around. Many children feared my mother.

Born in another region of Greece, she was the only outsider in the village. It wasn't just her outsider status. My mother didn't go to the Orthodox Church like the rest of the village. *She talked about the old gods as if they were family and friends. She had an altar and taught me how to call upon them. Some found her behaviors suspicious and many whispered "witch" behind her back. Some accepted her as a wise woman and healer. Others stepped out of her path, avoiding her at all costs, when she walked down the narrow street.*

She never minded their stares, their whispers, or them avoiding her. It made me angry, but she said there would come a time when the village and the whole world would once again believe in the gods.

She took me home, drew me a bath, gave me some dinner, and told me stories until I fell asleep...

... Late again, I was running for the bus. American schools were so far from your house. In Arachova, I could walk to school. That was before mom had to go back to Olympus. That was before dad remarried a villager.

The bus was pulling away.

I waved my arms, hoping the bus driver would see me and stop. Elation rippled through me when the breaks squeaked, giving my legs a burst of energy.

Marina and Dad are great, but I miss my real mother and Arachova. Dione wouldn't spend sixteen hours a day at a job and leave me to either take a bus to eat dinner or make what I could at home. I hate that she had to go back to Olympus, and I hated Zeus had that kind of power over her even more...

...The clinic nurse pulled the curtain behind her with one hand and held the chart with the other. Her eyes gave away the results before her lips uttered, "You're pregnant. Here are your options—"...

...Mom and dad were at the restaurant, as always, so it was easy to pack up what I needed. Still, my heart raced. I'm sure they'd support me through this, but not if they found out who I was having a child with. They'd left Greece to get me away from that life, from the cults popping up, worshiping the old gods. Anger built up inside, molten hot and ready to overflow. Like a daughter of a Titan would want to be an ordinary American girl.

Bags packed; I left the small home I'd known for the last time. Outside, she waited for me. The love of my life. We would be together forever, now...

... I cried into my pillow while the nurses took the baby to bathe. She didn't come. I was alone. No parents. No lover. Just my baby and me. Someone walked in and sat down. I didn't look up. It wasn't her. She left me to raise this baby, our baby, all on my own. Fucking gods. My parents were right. First, my mother Dione abandoned me, now—

"How would you like the power to make her pay. Make them all pay?"

I looked up and wiped my tear-soaked eyes with the back of my hand.

A man with curls and dark eyes that were awash with otherworldly power regarded me. He wore black pants and a grey button down, like a banker, who just took off his jacket and tie, except not modern. The conservative attire was way out of date in the 1970s. Yet, he pulled the look off. I didn't like men, not in that way, but he was so beautiful, I doubted he was a man at all. Just what I needed. Another immortal in my life. Great.

I stuck out my bottom lip. "Go away!"

He shook his head and clucked his tongue. "Not a very warm greeting for your grandfather."

"Nice try. I knew my grandfather."

I didn't know Dione's father. Considering he was either in Tartarus or banished to the void, I doubted this god was who he claimed to be.

He made a dismissive flick of his wrist. "Many, many generations ago, but you are the first worthy of my claim."

"Who are you? Zeus?" I didn't want the king of the gods in my life. At. All. He'd been horrid to my mother's other children, and he had a bad rap of having his way with anyone he pleased. Also, he wouldn't be pleased to discover who had given Apollonian this baby.

"I agree with your sentiments about my father. He's abused his power. He's the one who made your mother and your lover abandon you. We can stop his tyranny. Together."

I sat up, adjusting my blankets. "How so?"

"You will break the gates of Tartarus, by doing exactly the opposite of what your mother tells you to do."

... "I can't. I have a little girl," I protested. "I'm all she's got."

Not for the first time, Mother asked, "Who is her other parent?"

I shrug, burying the image of my love. "Nobody special."

"She has grandparents," Mother insisted, eyeing my small apartment with distaste. "Lydia will be better off with them. The job is too dangerous for a child."

I looked at my little girl, fast asleep. She didn't know when I tucked her in it would be the last time. Mother was right. This place was a dump. The folks could do better for her than I ever could if I didn't accept this Oracle position.

"You can visit her."

I shook my head. "No. It'll be too hard. It's better to make them all believe I died."

"That's not how we do it. Your father knows."

"I want her to have a normal life, okay? Leave her alone."

Dione regarded the sleeping child. "Are those your conditions?"

"Yes."

"As you wish."...

..."If I open the door, Lydia won't ever have to be oracle? She gets to keep living a normal life?" I asked.

The Titan is silent. However, the god nodded. "That's right."

I place my hands on the pillar.

TWENTY-SIX

A familiar scent filled my senses, a touch that I associated with massages and tender caresses, a voice that held a note of pleading, all of which brought me back to my body.

Hermes leaned over me while holding my hand. He smiled. "There you are."

"Apollo," I gasped, tears slid down my cheeks.

His dark eyebrows furrowed together, concern and confusion limning his features. He pointed to his chest. "I'm Hermes."

I waved my hand, sitting up. "No. No. I know who you are. Apollo tricked my mother into opening the gate a crack. She had second thoughts. He killed her."

"How do you know all this?" Athena asked.

Then, I explained that I connected with my ancestors' memories and how I could pluck the strings of their life and experience what they experienced, leaving out the bit where I discovered that Dione was my real grandmother. I had to sort through my own feelings about that, why I looked like the grandmother who raised me, and why Dione never said anything about it. "Apollo confessed to my mother that he wanted to open the gates of Tartarus. He wants to usurp his—your father's throne."

Hermes face darkened. There were other emotions brewing in his face as well.

"Sneaky little twerp," Hecate declared. "I better not have to come out of retirement."

Athena was the only one who didn't show a reaction. She held very still, but in her eyes, I could see that the goddess of wisdom was thinking. Hecate and Hermes watched her as well.

Finally, she spoke, "We cannot accuse Apollo with this information. A memory could be skewed or altered. We need to get him to confess."

"How will we do that?" I asked, though I'm sure we were all thinking it.

Athena smiled slightly. "Easily done. We appeal to his hubris with a false reading and a feigned reaction. You will falsely accuse someone of what he's done. Instead of punishment, they will receive all he wants."

It sounded like a good plan, but there were too many variables that could go wrong.

"That's a big con. Are we sure that we can get everyone to go along?"

Athena gave me an approving look as if she was proud of my question. "No need. Some discord will make the ruse appear more genuine. We simply need key gods to know and most of the rest will go along with their decision."

I snorted. Sounded like the gods were no different than humans when it came to running with the crowd.

"The only problem I see with the plan," Hecate said, a slight grimace on her face, "is that Apollo must have had supporters to think he could pull off such a grievous act."

"We'll weed them out in due time. The important thing is to unmask the mastermind behind all of this."

Hermes frowned.

"What's wrong?" I asked.

"My brother is no fool. I fear he won't react as you wish."

"It is a risk," Athena agreed. "Conversely, my plan is not as great a risk as accusing him outright and failing to prove anything. We have no other course of action, I'm afraid." Her gaze latched onto mine. "However, since you will shoulder the responsibility of the performance and risk to your personal safety, I shall leave it up to you to decide, Lydia."

All three waited patiently as I deliberated. Coming to a decision, I swallowed hard. "I'll do it."

Hecate grinned and rose. "Looks like I need to pack. Things are going to heat up on Olympus. I don't want to miss it!"

I PACED Hermes's chambers in the palace on Olympus while Athena worked the gods of this realm, Hermes notified Atlantis, and Hecate spoke with the king and queen of Hades about our plan. Lucinda patrolled the perimeter of the chambers. Cosmo stood guard by the door.

Arachne and Luke had joined us. We figured this would be the safest place for them while we confronted Apollo. The clicking of her knitting needles and the soft snore of my son, soothing sounds. I wished Nicky was here too.

The harpy queen stayed behind to gather the army on Earth. We wanted them ready to come to my call if our plan failed and a battle broke out. After weeks of training, I was ready to fight. I hoped.

Cerberus paced with me in his three-headed form. One head nudged my hand, needing pets. The other two heads panted, tongue lolling out of the side of their mouth. Viscous slobber dripped onto the floor. Used to the gross monster hound, I sidestepped his puddles with ease.

Hermes's sister was there. She wiped up the puddles until I told her that a sister shouldn't be a servant.

"I know." Her blue skin blushed purple. "I like taking care of Hermes's things while he's gone. It's the least I can do for the way he treats me."

"How is that?" Arachne asked.

"Like I'm of the ichor. He admits to everyone I'm his sister."

"You deserve to be treated well regardless of your bloodline."

I squeezed her free hand. Her blush deepened. The nymph murmured something and scurried off.

There was a knock on the door. Lucinda entered. Her face was stone cold, and her tone neutral as she announced, "King Zeus would like an audience with you." Her gaze darted to Arachne and Luke. "Alone."

My heart hammered against my rib cage, collective memories surfacing. He'd been many things to many women of my bloodline. I acknowledged the concern was my ancestors' and not my own, pushing it all down. He was a king, not my lover or friend or father— or *ick* all of the above.

"Come with me," Arachne said, waking my adult kid.

Luke rubbed his eyes with fisted hands like he did when he was small. My chest swelled with my love for my son. Luke gave me a questioning look.

"Zeus wants to speak to me alone." I added a smile to reassure him. "I'll be fine."

I took a seat, beckoning Cerberus to heel at my side. With a hand on the dog's head, I inhaled. On my exhale, I nodded to Lucinda.

The siren gave me a thumbs-up and returned to the entrance.

The king of the gods entered. Power rolled off him like crashing waves. I wasn't sensitive to it before, but I felt it now. No wonder he could defeat his father. I felt more raw energy coming off him than Hecate, and she was a daughter of a Titan, too.

I rose slowly.

"No need." He smiled that fatherly smile. It was there and gone. The king of the gods sat in a chair opposite mine. Apollo had sat in that chair the last time I'd been here. Zeus eyed me, taking in my measure as if for the first time.

"I once had a strong friendship with the Oracles," he began. "Some were my lovers. In a way, you and I are kin."

Thanks to generations of my family being left alone by gods, we were very distant kin. I nodded all the same, saying nothing. Revealing nothing. I'd seen enough clients over the years to know this was someone who had very few people he could confide in.

"You're a mother, so you must know the sorrow I feel to know my son believes he must walk the path I walked long ago."

Also, Zeus's father before him. Patricide was really popular among the ruling gods.

"Heavy is the head that wears the crown," I said in English, though he'd been speaking in Greek. I didn't want the meaning lost in translation.

"Shakespeare put it well, yes."

I blinked. I was surprised Zeus had even heard of the mortal.

Zeus ran his hand through his curls. Hermes got a lot of his beauty from his father. Yet, the father's flawless face and sculpted body did nothing for me. I knew too much.

"Unlike my daughter, I'm an old god. Not quick to violence as I had been in my youth. I don't want to lose my kin over this. Any of them." He sat straighter. "I need you to tell me the best path."

"I can only read the possibilities. Your chosen thread is up to you."

A sad smile curved his mouth. "You are like Dione, saying everything and nothing. I didn't know mortals of your era could be so wise. Tell me the future, Oracle." He held out his hand.

I placed mine in his and dove into the skein woven by the Fates without any aid other than my own ability. I picked three threads that glowed before me. There were numerous more that had a faint light, but I knew from my ancestors' experience that those threads were only slight variations of the trio and wouldn't be so different that it would matter. The three that glowed bright as those damned new-style headlights were three possibilities with greatly varied outcomes.

"Three threads. Three fates. The first of which means killing your progeny before they kill you. Their death will bring peace for now, death for all gods in a great war later. The second of which is killing the usurper, then mashing their ichor, bone, and flesh to feed to the gate of Tartarus. The supplication will seal the gate forever, but it will create doubt among your progenies. Who will you kill next? They will whisper. You and your brothers will die. The third thread is the one you will fight against the most, forever doubting your choice, but it is a sacrifice you must make."

I stopped. In a way, having control of my faculties sucked. He might take his anger over what I had to say out on me, and I didn't feel like fighting my boyfriend's father to the death.

Zeus leaned forward. "What is it, Lydia?"

He used my name. "Abdicate your throne, allow your progeny to rule, and the Titans to return to Othrys."

HERMES CRAWLED into bed next to me. His bed. Zeus's reading and soothing the god's subsequent temper tantrum had been emotionally and physically taxing. I had lain down directly after Zeus departed, only meaning to rest my eyes.

"Is it time?" I asked.

The messenger of the gods wrapped his arms around me from behind and kissed the back of my head.

"Not yet. Go back to sleep."

I settled into my pillow. More sleep sounded like an excellent idea. "Your dad is pissed at me."

"I don't think that's accurate. He just told me you were the best Oracle since the golden days and that he knows what he must do for the first time since the New Era."

The New Era was what the gods called the period since the

Supernatural Council of the Americas revealed that all supernaturals were real and a revival in the belief in the old gods surged.

"Did he happen to tell you what that would be?" I asked sleepily.

"No. That, he kept to himself."

I smiled to myself. "Your father is still worthy of ruling Olympus."

Hermes squeezed me. "You did something tricky, didn't you?"

Instead of answering, I snuggled closer and slipped back into sleep.

CHAPTER

TWENTY-SEVEN

Only once before had I been to the throne room in Olympus. The experience wasn't awesome. I wasn't connected to my oracular or harpy powers then and felt pushed and pulled. Today, I was here of my own accord to do something that would shape my, and everyone else's future.

The throne room was as grandiose as any palace on Earth with the added element of magic. Imposing marble columns, floors, and walls. Today, the ceiling was painted as an azure sky with the occasional cloud floating by. The entire Twelve sat on their thrones. The leaders of Atlantis and Hades brought entourages of seamen, sirens, and harpies.

Great. We'd need them.

Dressed in full Oracle regalia, I sat upon a tripod stool. I held my hands in my lap so I wouldn't fidget with the bracelets or jewelry. My head ached from the weight of the gold laurel crown and half of my voluminous curls piled on top of my head in an intricately braided bun.

The gods, nymphs, maenads, demigods, and other supernaturals assembled murmured to each other. I didn't know which ones

150

Athena convinced to go along with our ruse. She'd assured me those she'd selected were loyal to her and would influence the others.

At least, I knew the sirens, harpies, Persephone, Aidoneus, Poseidon, and the seamen were all on my side. I'd gotten no guarantees about Amphitrite. Poseidon had said he'd let his queen react naturally. I didn't know what that meant, but it'd seemed there might be a lack of trust there between the two.

According to Hermes, Zeus was on my side.

I'd warned Athena that Hera might be divided in her alliances because Dione had mentioned as much. Plus, we'd all seen Hera, Aries, and Apollo whispering on the recording of the council gathering. It may have been nothing. It may have been about everything.

"Thank you for the warning, but I wouldn't include Hera," Athena had responded. "My stepmother will react in whatever way benefits her the most. She's survived Kronos and my father. Be wary of Hera more than my brother Apollo."

As if the memory evoked her attention, Hera's gaze met mine. Or was it because I was looking at her too long?

I looked for Thanatos among the gods assembled. He was pretty easy to find. Most of the gods steered clear of the god of death, a concept that oddly frightened immortals much more than it did the short lived. There was no seeing past the darkness of his hood, but he waved and gave me a bony thumbs-up.

Ugh. Nice job, Captain Obvious.

It took all I had to not look in the direction of the Olympians to see if any noticed Thanatos's obvious cue. Annoying as death's thumbs-up was, at least I could breathe a little easier now that the backup plan was in place.

Athena left her throne and approached where I sat. She placed a hand on my shoulder. "The Oracle gave us all a prophecy that struck fear in our hearts not too long ago. Since then, all three realms of the brothers have experienced attacks, including our very own sacred space, Olympus."

The nervous excitement that spread throughout the room like a miasma, thickened into tension. Olympus, Atlantis, and the Underworld had known peace since the final Titanomachy—the war between the gods and Titans. That had been eons ago. The young gods had never known a threat. Maybe that's why Zeus bargained with the angels, to avoid a war that would cost more than it would be worth.

He did get a sweet deal though. Until recent years, most other pantheons were lost to obscurity or known by a few mythological studies majors. Whereas classical Greece and Rome, who revered Zeus (or Jupiter in the Roman tradition), were widely studied and known. Would the king of the gods truly give up his position just when the New Era had dawned and the chance to gain the power of belief of billions was at stake?

"We have gathered you all because she has found a way out of what we believed was inevitable."

In my periphery, I could see Zeus tense.

Arachne skittered across the dais holding a bowl of laurel leaves. Following her, Hermes's sister carried a bowl of liquid that reeked of sulfur and something else noxious. I didn't need the fumes or leaves anymore but didn't want to change the ceremony at this pivotal moment. I didn't need it, but as soon as I took a whiff, my eyes rolled back in my head.

I controlled the sight, plucking from the threads of the three paths. I made sure to have Apollo in my line of sight for his reaction as I gave the prophecy that I had given Zeus privately. While the rest of the throne room stared in awed silence, Apollo appeared positively gleeful as I spoke.

I hadn't told his father we suspected Apollo, but Zeus's gaze was also on his son. Did the king of the gods know all along that his favorite son was behind this? Was he the kind of parent who turned a blind eye to his child's faults until the kid did something truly egregious? Thinking about it, Zeus likely didn't see it coming because Apollo was most like him.

I finished, sweat beading on my forehead and out of breath.

Some of the crowd turned their gaze to Athena. It wasn't the false prediction Athena had planned. This was much better. It was the truth. Everyone murmured.

Zeus stood. "I have come to a decision. We will open the gates to Tartarus, and I will ab—" A thunderous boom cut him off. The palace shook. The ceiling erupted. Rubble and chunks of marble rained down.

Some gods shielded themselves with forcefields. Other beings ran for cover, including me. Fear and anger welled inside me as I ran away from the dangerous debris. Zeus almost had come to a decision on *my* advice, my prophecy. I had become an instrument of change, not a useless tool in other, more powerful beings' machinations.

Someone caught me by my waist. "It's me," Hermes shouted over the chaotic cacophony. He whisked me at a dizzying speed to the alcove where Nicky stood guard. Luke was inside, watching behind his harpy grandmother. We were soon joined by Arachne. In the alcove, the chaos was less and the ceiling intact.

"Everyone alright?" I asked after the wave of dizziness passed.

Nods all around.

Thanatos joined us. "There you are! Wow. Didn't expect the war so soon."

I frowned. "Guess Dione accepted the invitation to leave her prison to bear witness against Apollo with too much gusto."

Death shouted back, "Nah. I think this is someone else. Dione wasn't pissed that Apollo played her. She'd expected it."

Of course, my grandmother expected it. First Oracle knew all.

"Then who is attacking?" Athena's voice thundered from behind.

I swallowed hard. "One of Apollos's jilted conspirators. Since Thanatos doesn't think it's Dione, it's either Thetis or my mom." I sincerely doubted it was my mother since she was a fragment of who she'd been.

Athena scowled. "One is dead, lost to the Underworld. The other was eradicated."

"Nah, Thetis was part of it," Thanatos replied. "I found the judges in Tartarus. They told me."

"That would have been useful knowledge before the attack," Athena said the same thing as I was thinking. Outrage twisted Athena's beautiful face. "A nymph? A *dead* nymph has the hubris to think she can rule Olympus. *I* will end this." The goddess turned, full armor, shield and spear in hand.

CHAPTER

TWENTY-EIGHT

Athena was met with an army of undead. The rotting corpses of naiads spilled from the hole in the ceiling into the throne room. Twin-tailed melusinas, more bone than flesh, hissed and snapped from the entrances. Skeletal sea creatures with forgotten-by-me names piled in after them. It was as if Thetis called upon every manner of sea creature from the depths of Tartarus.

Thetis went straight for Apollo. As the two fought, Athena and his twin Artemis kept the others from attacking her brother. I didn't understand; he was the betrayer. Then again, his twin Artemis didn't know, and he wasn't attacking anyone but those attacking his kin.

Poseidon slammed his trident into the floor. Water burst in powerful springs, breaking apart the skeletons.

Zeus blasted the naiads with bolts of lightning. The parts that were not charred writhed and wriggled threateningly at their enemies. Hera, at her husband's side, created powerful miniature storms, casting them at the melusinas.

Ares barreled through scores of the undead, clobbering his way through with sheer force.

155

Hecate cast spells.

Sickle in hand, Thanatos reaped.

Back-to-back, Persephone and Hades worked as a cohesive unit blasting the dead with balls of shadows that sucked the undead up. My guess was to some sort of prison.

Each of the gods with the ability to fight, used their gifts. Others huddled in corners, protected by seamen and sirens, who fought against the incoming tide.

Cerberus was fighting off the undead, protecting me while I took in the scene. All three heads chomping bone and gross, rotten flesh.

Hermes entered the fray in his lethal godly form. Hermes flew near me, slicing and dicing faster than my eyes could track. Not going to lie, I liked the ferocity with which he fought. Not that I had much time to ogle him.

Arachne sent forth her children. A myriad of puppy-sized spiders swarmed a creature at a time. Arachne herself cast sticky nets trapping her victims. She unhinged her jaw. An inhumanly wide and long mouth with rows and rows of teeth devoured her prey.

I had to look away.

Some things were better as head-knowledge, but unseen.

"Call the harpies," Nicky said, fingers lengthening into sharp talons. "We'll need them."

I kicked off my sandals, allowing my own fingers and toes to grow into weapons. I drew my sword from the scabbard at my side. Finally, I released my wings and let out a harpy cry, entering the fray.

Luke screeched, bearing talons and a spike as his weapon of choice. He'd had months of training.

I only had weeks of practice, but hours upon hours of drills and sparring made a difference. I tore with my talons. Sliced with my sword, turning animated bone and rotten flesh to lifeless stone.

The undead seemed never ending. When we vanquished the lot, more came. How many naiads and enchanted creatures had died? More importantly, how did they die that they were so full of wrath and vengeance once raised from their graves?

I shrieked and wailed, calling the harpies to me. Even Nicky tried to call them. I felt the pull of her call myself. There was nothing wrong with our calls. The harpies around us, all looked our way. Something was very wrong back home, but there was nothing I could do about it if I stayed here. I flew above the battle, seeking out Luke.

"Luke!" I screeched.

The undead weren't attacking the sirens or harpies unless attacked. They weren't attacking Persephone or Hades. Hermes, they avoided as well. Hephaestus swung his hammer, and that seemed to be enough of a deterrent for the undead to leave him alone, too.

They concentrated on Zeus, Apollo, Poseidon, and Ares the most.

Those gods could handle themselves.

I couldn't see my son in the sea of bodies.

My heart leapt when I saw bright golden wings—Nicky, carrying an uninjured Luke.

Nicky joined me in the air with my son. I pointed out what I had seen. "They are seeking revenge, not the throne."

"I am bound to Hades. You are bound to Zeus and the Twelve."

"What about our sisters?"

She gave me a hard look. "They know their duty. If they're not here, they are fighting on another front. We can join them, but not until we are done here. Olympus is for the living, Lydia. They may be right in seeking justice for how they died. However, the imbalance, the *wrongness* of the undead in a place meant for the living, will destroy more than their intended target."

That, I understood.

This was our fight then.

"Are we going back in, ma?" Luke shouted.

"Yeah." I drew harpe again. "Let's finish this."

Nicky and Luke joined the harpies.

I didn't go to my sisters. I went straight for Thetis. The nymph didn't see me coming as I flew from behind and plunged harpe into her back. The supernatural blade sliced through bone and flesh hitting the heart. The petrification wasn't instant. Thetis turned to see her killer. A smile limned her features.

"I'm glad it was you." Her final words before the smile turned to stone.

Apollo pushed the petrified version of the undead nymph over. It cracked into a myriad of shards, crumbling to dust.

Poseidon let out a wail I've only heard from the recently widowed. The throne room trembled with the god's grief.

The rest of the undead army petrified and crumbled.

Hera held Zeus as he wept into his hands.

I was glad this didn't feel like a victory. Thetis was wrong to raise the dead, but they'd all been wronged. Only vengeance could power the sort of hatred to leave the peace of the afterlife to fight here.

Thanatos went to work, reaping the spirits of the dead before they could escape. Harpies grabbed onto shades with their claws, whisking them to their king. Hades worked magic, opening a door into his realm.

Hermes spun in a circle, rising. His wings and eyes turned black as a starless night. When he stopped spinning, an ebony cloak with silver trim unfurled and shrouded the god.

A tear of pride wet my cheek. He'd reclaimed the role of psychopomp. His first act, ushering the rest of the souls through.

Wrapped up in the death gods, I didn't notice the high beams had turned up on Apollo. He shone brighter than the few times I'd seen him. Obviously, he wasn't reading the room.

"Father! You said you would—"

"Hail the Oracle," Athena shouted, her voice louder than her brother's. She raised her spear. She grew brighter and brighter.

Dang. Athena literally *outshone* her brother.

She shouted, "Lydia Kourakos, savior of Atlantis! Lydia Kourakos savior of Olympus! All recognize the Harpy Queen who wielded the harpe of Perseus!"

The shouts roared, echoing within the walls of what was left of the throne room.

Outshone by his sibling and his descendant, Apollo backed away, loathing in his gaze.

A chilly frisson skittered up my spine like a thousand arctic spiders. The god slinking away could not be good. My fear was short lived, replaced by shock.

"My queen!"

A battered and bruised harpy from Nicky's flock stumbled into the throne room. Nora was in her arms. The priestess's skin was an ashen gray.

Athena ran to her worshipper, whisking Nora away. Hecate and Arachne joined her.

I sent a hope to whatever forces could help. I'd grown fond of Nora.

Once her burden was gone, the harpy announced her purpose, "Forgive us. We couldn't come to your call. Forces attacked Milagro Bay from the sea. We are losing."

TWENTY-NINE

When we arrived on Earth, we came upon a scene out of a Kaiju film. Monsters attacking a city's defenses. While Olympus faced an attack of the undead, Milagro Bay was beleaguered by every manner of *living* naiad, melusina, and creature of the sea that was once legend ... including Charybdis. I hadn't had the chance to see the Titan before. Not sure that I ever wanted to see a massive sea worm that likely outsized the sandworms of *Dune*.

While harpies fought the naiads and melusinas along the outskirts of the small town, the monster hurled the waters of the Strait of Juan de Fuca against the forcefield protecting the town. Someone with a lot of magic was sending bolts of pure energy at the barrier.

Soon after Hermes transported those of us who couldn't just meteor our way between worlds, fireballs that morphed into gods, followed.

A harpy broke ranks, flying directly to me and Nicky.

"Who's leading them?" I asked, without hesitation or allowing them to report.

"Amphitrite."

"What?" The stretch of wetland we stood upon quaked beneath my feet. It was the water responding to Poseidon's wrath. Amphitrite and Thetis, his wife and his lover had betrayed the god, and he was really in his feels about it.

Hera laughed without humor. "You all thought you could keep doing as you pleased regardless of our feelings? Now, you see us all pay, our worshippers pay because none of you could keep your hands to yourself."

"No one in Milagro Bay did a thing to them," I said, anger building up. "This is more than revenge." I pointed to the waves crashing against the magical forcefield. "Amphitrite wants attention. She wants to be feared and revered like the gods of old."

Lucinda stepped forward. "The problem is the mundane authorities called the International Supernatural Enforcement Agency have made it clear they didn't want us to bring our troubles here. Since you didn't bring her to the meeting, your wife doesn't know, does she?"

Poseidon gripped his trident. "I'll stop her before it's a problem."

The trident glowed. Thousands of phallic eels and dolphin ships burst onto the scene, hovering above. In another situation, the aerial penis parade would have brought me to tears, laughing. Now, we needed all the help we could get.

The god of the sea pointed toward the melee. The eels and dolphins took action.

Hades held up his bident. It glowed. Innumerable harpies swarmed the sky above, descending into the fight their sisters were losing.

Persephone nodded to Lucinda. The siren general, transformed into her beautiful, feathered form.

Every gaze turned to her, enthralled, except me and Nicky. Harpies must be immune. Since I was in my harpy form, I must have been granted immunity.

More sirens, all beautiful and powerful filled the sky heading for Charybdis. "I must join my sisters," Nicky said.

Luke looked to me, but I was waiting for Athena, Ares, or even Zeus to give a command for an attack. I could fight one on one, but I wasn't sure if I could stab Charybdis here. A giant worm statue might raise some eyebrows, even in the quirky Pacific Northwest. Surely, the gods had means of capturing and transporting her out of here.

None of the gods made a move.

"Why isn't anyone *doing* anything?" I asked. I wished Athena was here or Hecate, but they stayed to tend to Nora and the wounded harpy.

No one replied. The gods all stood there like powerful, immovable statues. Hermes didn't even look at me. Zeus turned to me, his face an unreadable mask. His eyes though. His eyes were filled with impotent rage. Yet, he didn't explain himself.

Hera blew out her breath. "We're not allowed to interfere on this plane. Not with something this ...visible."

I shook my head, unable to comprehend. "You're gods. You rule your own realms, you fought and imprisoned the Titans. The angels were weakened when the council came out. Who are you afraid of?"

Then it clicked in my mind. Gabriel had said that ISEA would release the effects of mundane belief on supernaturals. The gods were afraid of losing the power human worship gave them. Would they cease to exist? Or were they afraid they'd be like I was before I had my powers, weak and normal?

Didn't the gods realize that wasn't the end of the world? Cognitive dissonance would prevent some mundanes from believing the study. Conspiracy theorists would come up with reasons why the study was meant to control, not free people's minds. I felt pity for them. All that magic, all those eons of existence, and they were afraid of mortals—more importantly they were afraid of becoming irrelevant.

I'd spent my whole life being irrelevant. I had no fear of obscurity.

"Well, I'm allowed. So are you, if you'd rather be a hero than a deity ruling from afar," I said, glancing in Hermes's direction.

Instead of joining me, the god looked down. Disappointment bloomed in my chest, poisonous and sharp petals. My eyes burned. I was used to so many people disappointing me, but not Hermes. He'd always come to my rescue despite the rules, even when I was a child.

I spun away. I couldn't look at him. Not now. I needed my courage, not my hurt.

"Please," Poseidon begged. "Don't kill her."

I turned to face the god. "I don't want to kill Amphitrite, but I will if that is the only way to stop her."

He shook his head. "Charybdis. She wasn't always a monster." He glanced at his brother. Zeus produced a singular manacle of burnished gold. "Touch her with this, and she'll no longer be a threat to your home."

I glared at him, taking the manacle and stuffing it into a sac. It would be much easier for a full god than someone with human, harpy, and a Titan mix of magic. I pushed off, taking flight.

I didn't fly directly at Charybdis or Amphitrite. I wanted an aerial view, away from the gods and their disappointing limitations, so I could think.

The sirens attempted to sing to Charybdis, lulling the massive worm creature. Only problem with that was she proved to be immune, by inhaling and chomping down on a group of sirens unable to fly away in time.

Horrified by the site, I cried out. All those lives gone because the gods wouldn't lift a finger.

Even with a good number of sirens distracting Charybdis, I didn't know if I could get close enough to touch her with a manacle let alone stab her with my sword cursed with Medusa's blood without getting sucked in.

I searched the beach, looking for Amphitrite. Maybe I couldn't get the biggest threat, but at least I could stop the goddess.

There! Along the shore, Amphitrite sent a blast of raw magic to weaken the wards that created the forcefield. She seemed to concentrate with her whole being on the effort. Anger twisted the goddess's features into a mask of rage. The queen of Atlantis couldn't figure out why her old and powerful magic couldn't just break simple wards.

Not so easy, is it?

Nicky told me the magic guarding the supernatural town was older than her. That Milagro Bay was founded by supes indigenous to the Pacific Northwest. The wards relied upon the magic of the land itself and the blood and bones of the creatures who were born, had lived, and died here. Though known throughout the world. Amphitrite was a goddess with a nominal number of believers. The fact that the goddess could breach the forcefield powered by the wards at all was a miracle. It had to be her power and Charybdis's combined.

A group of helicopters approached from a distance. I heard them before I saw the formation. *Shit.* Western Washington was home to several military bases.

Charybdis turned toward the sound, roaring.

"Okay she's given you a warning, soldiers. Stay back," I muttered. My gaze dipped to Amphitrite. She seemed oblivious she'd gotten the attention of this world's military. Morbidly, I wondered if she would survive a missile to the head. Our weapons weren't what they used to be.

The problem was they wouldn't stop with who *I* thought were the bad guys. We were all monsters to them. They'd bomb the sirens and harpies, maybe even the gods, if they didn't do the cowardly thing and return to their realm.

The helicopters continued their approach.

Shit. Shit.

I wavered. I could attack Amphitrite and end this, or I could save or stop the soldiers in the helicopters—whatever they were packing wouldn't do us any good and could get them killed.

The dilemma was solved for me when sirens broke away from the rest who'd survived Charybdis. Lucinda was leading them.

The Titan may be immune to siren song, but I doubted the soldiers were. With the sirens flying toward the helicopters and their voices trailing on the wind, I knew I had to get to Amphitrite.

I had a hunch that the goddess was controlling the Titan and had also controlled Scylla. Why else would an ancient being attack a place that had nothing to do with her imprisonment?

I stayed in the air, partly watching the sirens approach the incoming helicopters and Charybdis thrashing and attempting to suck up the sirens left behind, but mainly focusing on Amphitrite, waiting for her to put her full concentration on blasting another wave of magic.

When she did, I dove. I'd practiced the blow I served the goddess a hundred times a day for weeks. I practiced on dummies. I practiced with a wooden sword on Nicky. She came at me with plenty of counter attacks. Part of me feared it wasn't enough. Most martial artists, most soldiers get more training, right? Didn't Luke Skywalker spend years with Yoda?

I was waffling.

It wasn't me failing that I was afraid of. I didn't want to kill a person. Wasn't Scylla a person? A weird, monster-shaped giant person, but hadn't she once been a being like Amphitrite? I couldn't remember her story. Not now, not with all the pressure. I had seconds to decide.

There were children in Milagro Bay. There were children around the world. Amphitrite wouldn't stop at one place, she'd keep going. Anyone bent on power through force never stopped at one city. My own kid was down there. Juan could be taking the train or sitting in our house watching in horror.

No. I couldn't let Amphitrite do this.

She wasn't going to harm one person, she'd slay many.

Mind made up; I dove. Outrage that she'd try to take over my town, my life, my world, building until I was my anger. I never touched her with my sword. All that was in me that wanted to protect hurled from my talons in a surge of lightning. I struck the goddess with all I had, smiting an immortal with my Titan gift from my grandmother.

A pile of ash lay upon the ground where Amphitrite had stood. I'd killed a god. I annihilated a god.

I'd killed a person.

Horror and wonder married in my chest, a nightmarish wedding. I wish I had time to contemplate, to mourn, but suddenly I was falling upwards, sucked by the current created by Charybdis's gargantuan gaping maw.

CHAPTER

THIRTY

I couldn't fight against the current sucking me in. I wasn't afraid. A calm acceptance washed over me, slowing time and allowing me to say goodbye. I killed and now I'd be killed. I'd die but at least I'd stopped Amphitrite from destroying my home, my new friends, my son, and the man I'd hoped would one day be my son-in-law, Juan. My only regret is that I'd trusted another man who'd let me down.

I didn't want to admit it, but I'd done more than trust Hermes. I'd fallen in love with the god over the past few months. How sad that I just realized it now when his betrayal hurt the worst.

Something slammed into me, altering my course. Breath flew out of my lungs in a loud *whoosh*. I gasped for air. A steel embrace held me fast. Once I caught my breath, relief washed over me.

Hermes's face, a breath from mine. Grim determination plastered on his sculpted features, as we hurtled through the sky away from Charybdis and up. We moved so fast, I couldn't see anything but Hermes and my own body.

"The manacle," he shouted.

Stunned, it took me a moment to register what he wanted from

167

me. Coming to my senses, I rummaged through the bag one-handed. Hermes held me too tightly to do anything else. My fingers gripped old, circular metal. A ring. A manacle.

"Got it!"

"Do you trust me?"

Did I trust him? I shared my bed and my life with him—didn't I do the same with Carlo for so much longer. I didn't trust my ex. My ex hadn't gone through the lengths Hermes had. Hadn't put himself between me and a Titan like Hermes did when he faced Typhon. Carlo hadn't put himself in front of a monster capable of swallowing a large cruise ship let alone us. My ex-husband ran from me as soon as he had more than I could give him.

Hermes had enough. I could never give him anything he didn't already have, but he wanted me. *Loved* me.

"I do."

"We're going to fly so fast that you won't be able to see, but I want you to hold the manacle out and trust that I won't get us killed."

"Okay."

A smile lit his face like sunlight peeking through the clouds on a dismal day. A symphony played in my head. In that moment, I knew that I'd fallen for Hermes despite my guardedness, despite all the disappointment and heartache I suffered, because I was still me. A person who was capable of loving and being loved in return. Carlo's mistreatment hadn't taken that from me.

Hermes mouth crashed into mine, letting me know he felt exactly the same as I did. The kiss was everything, passion, romance, and a promise that he'd give me many more for a long, long time. An eternity, if I wanted.

He broke off the kiss. "Ready?"

"As I'll ever be."

He smiled. "That's my sweet potato."

I chuckled. "Sweet potato?"

"I'm trying pet names. You don't like it?"

I chuckled again. "If we live, I'll let you know."

His smile faded. "We'll live. We must. I want a life with you here, and I've never wanted something so much."

"Alright then. Hermes wants it. So, we'll live."

"I'm glad you see things my way. Ready?"

"I am, carrot."

A grin once again touched his lips, wide enough to dimple his cheek. "Hold tight and close your eyes. I'm going to go as fast as I can go."

To fight the vertigo of moving faster than I've ever moved, I held out the manacle and closed my eyes. My ears popped and then rang. My eyes felt like they were going to implode. Capillaries burst in my nose. Blood gushed. Some of the warm metallic liquid seeped between my lips pressed together in a determined grimace.

I didn't touch Charybdis with the manacle. My fist thrust into the giant worm's hide, breaking through to warm and wet flesh. Pain jolted up my arm, and I felt and heard the crunch of my bones despite the constant ringing in my ears. I screamed the whole time.

"Let go of it," Hermes shouted.

I did as he asked.

He pulled on me, until my arm was free. He flew away until I guessed we were at a safe distance. It was then I dared to open my throbbing eyes.

Charybdis shrank. Shrank might not be the right word. Flesh collapsed into itself until there was no more massive worm. Just as Charybdis winked out of existence, the corners of my vision folded in on themselves until I was submerged in darkness.

CHAPTER

THIRTY-ONE

When I woke in my room in my own bed, I almost thought I'd dreamt the whole thing. The cast on my arm and the dull pain in my face let me know none of it was imagined.

Hermes stayed by my side, bringing me my meals, fetching me drinks, bathing me, and taking me to the toilet. I could walk, but the mortal part of me wasn't made for the speed the god had traveled let alone the impact.

Hecate told me I would've died if Dione wasn't my grandmother. Funny that. Being Dione's granddaughter put me in danger in the first place.

The naiads and melusina lost their enthusiasm when their queen and the Titan were killed and imprisoned. They surrendered and were taken to a special place Hades made in the Underworld just for them. They'd be tried in what would be three thousand Earth years. If found guilty, they would be executed. It was Poseidon's hope they'd be contrite by then and come to live in Atlantis.

He needed a new queen, after all.

Thanatos had found the judges in Tartarus. They told him that

Thetis had been behind the attacks and Amphitrite had come to the dead water nymph to make a deal. The two plotted to capture me to open the gates. That's why they were attacking Milagro Bay. They had no idea I was in Olympus during the initial attack. Poseidon had thought it was suspicious that his wife had just let Charybdis go, let alone came back unharmed.

I was more than an Oracle and a harpy. I was a Titan. As one generation removed from Dione, I had more magical juice than Amphitrite. Go figure.

No one talked about who *killed* Thetis in the first place. Well, they did, but it was behind closed doors.

Current problem solved; Zeus didn't act on my prophecy. He would not abdicate the throne. He wouldn't hear of Apollo's involvement from Athena. The gates to Tartarus were still closed.

All that we went through, and we were in the same position.

Thanks to my Titan blood, my healing went quickly. I was out of the cast and completely ambulatory within a week.

Other changes happened during that time. Luke decided he wanted to give his life with Juan in West Seattle a try again. With the permission of the archangel, he packed his things while I recovered and was leaving this morning.

My son was a grown man. He wanted normalcy, or what would serve as normalcy after discovering his powers and the extent of the dangers of the supernatural world. He would come down twice a month on the weekend to train at the gymnasium and serve at the temple.

The temple. I hadn't been there, and I wasn't sure if I wanted to. Apart from Hermes, and Athena who had been tending Nora, I was disappointed in the Olympians, binding contract or no.

The Supernatural Council of the Americas had covered the event. The soldiers in the helicopter all reported seeing exactly what they were told they saw: a training exercise for supes.

I rose early, showered and got ready on my own. Hermes woke sometime during and got ready faster than I did. I winced when he sped past me. Not that I was afraid of him. I knew how much it hurt when you crashed at those speeds.

He paused behind me in the bathroom mirror, arms snaking around me from behind.

"Are you sad?" He whispered, his breath fanning my ear and cheek.

I nodded.

His hands slid up my sides. "Want a distraction?"

"Definitely." I grinned, loving the feel of his hands on me. Those hands had cared for me, but I wanted them to do other things now that I was healed. "After they leave? I want as much time with Lukie and Juan as I can."

"Call him Luke. You know he prefers it," Hermes chastised, smoothing things over with a peck on my cheek.

How could just a peck from him cause so many butterflies and *heat?*

I mimicked a world-weary sigh. "Alright, alright. I'll call him Luke."

"Race you downstairs?"

"Ha ha."

He was gone in a flash.

On the stairs, I was met by Gregory, one of Arachne's spiders the size of a puppy. He spun in a circle on the landing. A yellow sticky note was on his back.

I wasn't getting out of taking it off his body. I'd plunged my arm into the eyeball and flesh of two monsters, but spiders still gave me the creeps.

I took the two steps that would bridge the distance between Gregory and me, taking the sticky note as quickly as one would rip off a Band-Aid.

I'm going to live with Athena for a while. We've decided to give it another try. Take care of our kids while the moms kiss and make up.

xo, Arachne

"What? I wouldn't know the last thing about taking care of spider babies!"

Twin peals of laughter rang from the top of the stairs.

"Gotcha!"

Arachne and Athena, bored immortal pranksters. Even the still-healing Nora chuckled behind them.

I grinned and threw the wadded-up sticky note at them. I was grateful for their nonsense. My mood had been a little dark with Luke and Juan leaving.

Downstairs, Juan and Luke waited, coats on and bags already in Nicky's car. She would drive them to the train station.

I hugged and kissed my son and maybe future son-in-law—although I already considered Juan family.

"Before we leave, we have something to tell you," Luke began.

Juan took my hand. "We're getting married this summer."

"You set a date?" I smiled ear to ear.

"We did," they replied in unison.

I hugged my son and his fiancé again, so happy for them I could burst.

Behind them, Hermes smiled. His dark eyes met mine, setting my insides ablaze and melting my knees. I could see all the things he wanted to do to me once the boys left in that look.

Everything wasn't alright, not by a long shot, but we had good things coming our way to look forward to.

And as for the problems? We'd face them together.

Acknowledgments

I'd like to thank my editing team, cover artist, ARC readers, and readers. Without your support, these books wouldn't exist.

I'd like to thank my cat, John. Thanks for sitting on my shoulder. Your butt warmed my arthritic joint so I could write longer. You're the real MVP. Also, if you're reading this, can you let me know you can write as well as read?

You spend an awful lot of time looking confused and meowing at walls. It might help to write out where the hidden doors are, or how the wall has offended you so that we can better assist you.

About the Author

T.J. Deschamps is an author of Paranormal Women's Fiction, Urban Fantasy, and Fantasy. She lives in the Seattle suburbs with her kids, cats, and a tortoise.

Reading, dancing, and word games have always been the ways she prefers to spend her time. She lifts weights and exercises for her health (and hates every minute of it). As she approaches her fifties, she gardens. Her propensity to kill house plants has not continued in the outdoors.

ALSO BY T.J. DESCHAMPS